THE FRINGE SERIES

"Best science fiction I have read in a long while."
~Michael D. Griffiths, *SF Reader*

"*Fringe Runner* is epic fun with great characters, action, and suspense. Rachel Aukes is the next big name in the Space Opera genre!"
~ Nicholas Sansbury Smith, best-selling author of the *Extinction Cycle* series

"A perfect read for fans of the fantasy and sci-fi genres."
~ Ethan Gregory, *One Guy's Guide to Good Reads*

"I would recommend this novel to anyone who likes action-filled space operas and stories about fighting against the ruling government."
~ *Audiobook Reviewer*

EARTH UNDER SIEGE

"...Everything I've come to expect from this author. It's packed full of action, drama, surprise and suspense at every turn."
~*Silvia at Goodreads*

"Highly Recommended. Five Mysterious Stars."
~*RBS Productions*

"A top ten book!"
~ *Step into Fiction*

THE DEADLAND SAGA

Included on Suspense Magazine's "Best of 2013" list

Listed by the Huffington Post as one of the Best Zombie Books

"100 Days in Deadland is a stunning exploration of the human spirit: survival and greed, good and evil...a microcosm of today's society wrapped up in a dystopian novel. Rachel Aukes has written a modern take on a classic. I for one, cannot wait for her next book."
    ~ *Suspense Magazine*

"Another great zombie survival book made its way to our hungry brains! The book never slows down, the events are unpredictable and the characters are well built.... So go get the book, you'll love this one!"
    ~ *Zombie-Guide Magazine*

"This book is 5 stars all the way. It is unlike any zombie or apocalyptic story I have ever read... *100 Days in Deadland* doesn't just tell a story about zombies, it tells a story about a person's struggle to survival in a world that has fallen apart and how that person grows and changes through it all."
    ~ *Horror Web*

"A great read about survival in an undead world."
    ~ *Buy Zombie*

FRINGE WAR

SERIES BY RACHEL AUKES

Waymaker Wars

Space Troopers

Flight of the Javelin

Bounty Hunter

Fringe Series

The Deadland Saga

FRINGE WAR

FRINGE SERIES
BOOK 4

RACHEL AUKES

WAYPOINT BOOKS

WAYPOINT BOOKS

For Brian, always.

CONTENTS

CHAPTER 1

TIPPING POINT

Rebus Station, Terra

THE FIVE BLUE-SKINNED Myrads quickened their pace as they made for their hotel in Rebus Station.

Nannette, one of the two women in the group, threw a hurried glance over her shoulder. "There's another one back there now. They're definitely following us."

"Quit looking back," Edmun said. "They're probably just drunk and looking for an excuse to pick a fight." While he spoke, he scrolled through the functions on his wrist comm and tapped the *Emergency* icon.

After several seconds, a comm tech's face appeared on the small screen. *"Emergency services. How may I assist you, Citizen Edmun Strand?"*

"We're being followed by some colonists," Edmun said. "Can you send help?"

"I have a squad of dromadiers three blocks from your location. I am sending them your locator ID now. They should be there within two minutes."

Edmun let out a breath. "Thank you." He scanned his group, giving them a reassuring nod. "You hear that? They'll be here in no time."

The group didn't slow down, and neither did the three colonists following them. Four more colonists emerged around the corner ahead, walking straight toward the Myrads.

Edmun slowed and then abruptly cut to the right, taking his group off the sidewalk to cross the street.

"They're all following us," Nannette said, her voice a couple octaves higher than normal.

Yet another group of colonists emerged from an alley across the street. Edmun froze, then spun around to see himself and his friends trapped in the middle of the street as the groups converged around them.

"Let me handle this," Edmun announced to his friends, all of whom were wide-eyed and stiff with fear. He turned to face the colonists and held out his hands in a non-threatening manner. "Listen, we don't want any trouble. We're with the Citizens Against Hunger Program. CAHP is a humanitarian group. We're here to help you."

"Ha!" One of the colonists stepped forward. He was dirty, and his hair looked like it'd gone years without a cut. He was dressed, like his compatriots, in frayed brown clothes and an over-sized, heavy canvas coat. "We wouldn't be hungry if it wasn't for you *citizens* taking half our food and ninety percent of our income."

The ice in the leader's glare brought chills across Edmun's skin. He swallowed. "If you need credits, we don't have much, but we'll give you what we can."

"Can you make the droms leave us alone?"

"The Collective Unified Forces exists to protect everyone in the system," Edmun said, hoping the CUF's dromadiers would be there soon to rescue them.

"Bullshit. All they do is beat us and take our kids." The leader opened his coat and pulled out a rifle. "The Collective taking everything of ours stops today."

Gasps and whimpers came from Edmun's group. He felt a trickle of sweat roll down his face. The weapon wasn't a photon gun—it was something much older—but he knew it was likely just as deadly.

The group of colonists had moved to form a V in Edmun's line of sight. With the area behind him now opened, his first instinct was to turn and sprint away. Maybe that was what the colonists wanted—to watch citizens turn tail and run. But he was a Myrad, and Myrads weren't mongrels that ran at the first sign of danger. He inhaled deeply to tamp down his fear. The droms would be here any second. All Edmun had to do was buy his group time. "Listen," he began. "You don't want to do this. They'll throw you in prison for twenty years if you hurt a citizen. Take our credits. If that's not enough, I have a ship at the docks—"

The leader raised his rifle.

"No!" Nannette cried out.

The man fired. A loud blast echoed off the building walls around them.

Someone screamed.

Edmun felt an incredible pressure in his chest. He looked down to see a dark stain. He lifted a hand to the spreading stain and numbly discovered a puncture wound just above his heart. The pain hit him then, excruciating agony that dropped him to his knees. He tried to suck in a breath but couldn't find any air. Panic took control. He gasped, but his inhalations never reached his lungs.

Around him, a cacophony of gunfire erupted. He wanted to scream for help, but his mouth filled with tangy liquid. He coughed and sputtered for only a moment before everything faded into floating darkness.

CHAPTER 2

HOW WAR IS MADE

Parliament, Myr

CORPS GENERAL BARRETT ANDERS stood behind the podium facing the emergency Parliament session on Myr. He could've addressed the members with the formality they were used to, but instead decided to go with the straightforward approach. "By now, you should've read the terms of the cease-fire agreement. As part of those terms, I request Parliament to declare the fringe planets as independent worlds of the Collective, with guaranteed open trade through all four fringe stations, to be detailed via individual trade negotiations."

The senators raised an uproar. Voices stepped on one another as politicians declared their dissent.

Anders let them carry on for a minute before speaking loudly into the microphone. "Tell me why each planet within the Collective shouldn't be treated equally."

"Because they're colonies, not citizen-states," someone yelled. "Those colonies wouldn't exist without our resources and support."

Anders held back a shrug. "Myr and Alluvia were Earth's colonies as well, yet Earth never once dictated control after the colony ships left Earth's system."

"The fringe worlds don't have the infrastructure to manage themselves. They need us," another called out.

"Do they?" Anders looked across the faces until he found who he sought. "What do you have to say about that, Senator Finnegan? As the sole representative of the colonies to Parliament, do you believe they are capable of managing themselves?"

The senator, a plump, elderly man, took his time to turn on the microphone at his table. "I do believe the colonies are capable of managing themselves," he drawled out.

"You have to say that for your constituents or else you won't get voted in next term," a senator shouted.

Finnegan held up a hand. "However, each fringe world was settled by colonists with Collective backing. It was the Collective —namely, Myr and Alluvia—that provided the funds and resources to establish each new planet's first colonies, which became what we know as the fringe stations. As such, I believe two things must be made true for the Collective to thrive. First, I believe the fringe worlds should remain in the Collective as independent citizen-states. After all, it's natural evolution for colonies to mature. We all know the Collective would collapse if four of its six worlds broke free. We learned a hard lesson when the blight was released at Sol Base, which cut us off from over half of the Collective's food supplies for several months. That brings me to my second belief. I have long been a proponent for allowing multiple fringe stations on each planet as redundancies, with each world managing its own docks, just as Myr and Alluvia do today. I believe today is the day we lift the ban on the fringe worlds and allow them to build and manage their own space docks."

Anders suspected the fringe was already building space

docks under the Collective's nose. He'd dispatched drones to orbit all four fringe worlds to detect any such construction, but space docks only needed silo openings for ships to be launched. Finding holes with diameters of less than one hundred fifty meters wide equated to finding the proverbial needle in the haystack.

"Then the fringe would control the docks," a senator called out.

"If they control the docks, they can dictate trade terms and tax us for landing," another said.

"True enough," Finnegan said. "However, capitalism creates competition, which will ensure equitable rates for everyone. The CUF has controlled the docks for too long. Don't you agree, Corps General?"

"Absolutely," Anders replied quickly, thankful to get the floor back from the famously long-winded senator. "If the Forces were freed up from maintaining the status quo within the Collective, then we could focus on the future, such as exploring for habitable systems for expansion. That, I believe, would be a boon to everyone."

Anders noticed movement from the corner of his eye. He looked to see a senator from Alluvia stand and proceed toward the podium. He grimaced inwardly. Gabriel Heid was the well-known co-chair of Parliament and was believed to have much of Parliament already in his back pocket.

Anders had gone through the Academy with the senator's daughter. He and Gabriela Heid had become friends, staying in touch even after she stole the warship she commanded and joined the fringe cause. He'd seen firsthand how Senator Heid treated his daughter like a disposable pawn, always using her to improve his career. The senator was a snake, and Anders did not trust him.

Anders didn't move from the podium when Heid came to a stop right next to him.

Heid bumped Anders—no doubt, intentionally—as he leaned close to the microphone. "While I believe all this discourse is interesting, it distracts us from the crucial decision we must weigh today. The violence we've seen in the colonies has gone too far. We must take measures to end the rebellion taking place across the fringe worlds."

"I don't see how that discussion is any different from the one we're having now, Senator," Anders said. "I have negotiated a cease-fire with Seda Faulk to bide time for Parliament to establish equitable terms for all six worlds. Seda Faulk declared that anything other than the independence of colonies is a non-negotiable outcome. The sooner Parliament acknowledges their independence, the lower the risk we have of the cease-fire being violated."

"I'm afraid it's too late for that, Corps General," Heid said.

Anders frowned. "What do you mean?"

Heid glanced at him briefly before turning to face Parliament. In that brief moment, Anders could've sworn he'd seen smugness in the older man's face.

"Less than one day after the torrents blew up one of our destroyers, they attacked innocent citizens. Three hours ago, five Myrads, who were on a CAHP humanitarian mission, were slaughtered on Rebus Station."

The room burst into another uproar. Gabriel Heid tamped down the air and waited for the members of Parliament to quit talking among themselves. He continued. "The CAHP killings prove the fringe has no intention of respecting a cease-fire."

"I will ensure justice is done," Anders said. "Once I review the footage—"

Heid held up a hand. "I think you've done enough already, Corps General. You've given the fringe rebels validation that if they kill citizens, you'll give in to their demands. They've been behaving like unruly children and will continue to throw tantrums as long as it gets them what they want. I say we treat them like children and rein them in."

Parliament broke out into cheers.

Anders steamed. He shot a glare at Heid before turning back to the room. "Then you will fight another war, as bloody, if not more so, like the one Myr and Alluvia fought before forming the Collective." With that, he stepped down from the podium and returned to his seat on the floor.

Heid placed both hands on the podium, claiming it. "Corps General Anders says we'll have war, and I agree. I believe he's taken us to a point where there is no turning back. The fringe has shown an utter disregard for life with first the blight and now the CAHP killings. When they murdered Corps General Ausyar and killed everyone on board the *Unity*, Corps General Anders not only did *not* punish those responsible, he negotiated terms in their favor. We need to show the colonists that they are a part of the Collective, and that the Collective does not stand for mass murder. I move to immediately and definitively declare war on the colonies."

Parliament became louder than at any time earlier in the session. The few dissonant shouts were drowned out by cheers.

"All colonies? Darius hasn't shown aggression," a senator yelled through her microphone to speak over the cacophony.

"If we leave a single colony, the rebels will relocate there," Heid said, the room quieting at his voice. "The Space Coast isn't part of the Collective, and that asteroid belt has long been home to criminals. If the rebels choose to move there and away from the good people of the Collective, I'd say we let them."

Senator Finnegan tapped his microphone. "War is unnecessary. I will speak with my constituents. I'm sure we can reach an agreement."

"The time for negotiations is over," Heid said. "The Collective, by its very name, must be unified."

Cheers erupted.

Heid continued. "I loathe violence—as I know you all do—but pain is sometimes the only way to get through to an obstinate mind. If the colonies hurt enough, their minds will open to the truth that the Collective serves everyone. Therefore, I propose we accept the war the colonies have been asking for and initiate wartime law over all four colony worlds."

Senator Etzel, Parliament's co-chair from Myr, stood. "I second your proposal, Senator."

Heid nodded. "How say you all, senators?"

All the members, save three, raised their hands and shouted their agreement. Anders felt nauseous.

"The ayes have it," Heid said. "Effective now, the Collective is fighting a civil war against criminals spreading lawlessness across the four colony worlds."

The senators responded with cheers, and Anders couldn't mistake the arrogance in Heid's expression when the senator turned his gaze to him. Heid practically smiled before he turned back to face Parliament.

"Further, I believe we all want this war to be as short-lived as possible and to minimize costs to the Collective in terms of resources and loss of life. To accomplish that, I believe we need a Corps General who is up to the task. Barrett Anders has proven he cares more about placation than peace. I propose Commandant Maximus Laciam, commander of the freshly repaired *Unity*, to serve the Collective as Corps General, and Barrett Anders be removed from his current command as Corps General of the Collective Unified Forces and commandant of the *Littorio*, and be demoted to commandant of a destroyer-class ship within the *Unity*'s complement. There, Anders may still provide value to the Collective while under the leadership of a commandant not afraid to face problems head-on."

Anders scowled. Heid had complete control of Parliament, and he knew it. But naming Laciam? That arrogant Myrad was at least a decade away from having the skills and experience to serve as Corps General of the CUF. Anders could list at least twenty better-qualified candidates. Anders had met Laciam when the lad was first officer on Gabriela Heid's *Arcadia*. Laciam and a dozen other dromadiers, who'd been unwilling to follow her to fight for the fringe, had been dropped onto a transport ship and left floating in space for a week until they were picked up by one of Ausyar's ships. That Heid was naming Laciam meant Laciam was as much a puppet as Ausyar had been.

"I concur, Senator Heid," Senator Etzel said. "I feel the interests of the Collective will best be served by a Corps General who's dedicated his entire career to serving the Collective. I have met Max Laciam. He comes from a long line of stalwart defenders of the Collective."

Anders noticed how good Heid was at acting humble, though anyone who'd ever met him would know the man was the opposite.

Heid spoke. "You have heard our recommendation. "How say you all, senators?"

Nearly all the Alluvians and Senator Finnegan did not raise their hands.

Heid looked across the room. "The ayes have it. Thank you, Senators, friends. You have equipped our military to fight the war swiftly and adeptly."

The room broke out in cheers and applause once again.

Anders shook his head in disbelief. He stood and strode from the room. He tried to ignore the cheers until the door shut behind him, granting him silence. Gabriel Heid now controlled both Parliament and the CUF, making him essentially an emperor.

Anders had at first believed Heid wanted a war. Now, he understood it was power that Heid had been after all along. Heid had needed the war to run a power play he'd clearly been planning for some time. He wondered how long it would be before Heid eliminated the concept of a Corps General.

Despite Heid's political games, Anders knew that securing victory in a civil war was another story.

Anders had seen the passion for independence across the fringe, passion that Heid was blind to. Myr and Alluvia had treated the colonists as second-class people for too long. The Collective may have the technology, but the colonists outnumbered the citizens ten to one, and the colony worlds had far more raw resources. The longer the war dragged out, the more Myr and Alluvia would suffer. Anders wondered if Heid had considered the likelihood of the fringe winning the war? Because Anders certainly had, and he was starting to believe it would be the better outcome.

CHAPTER 3

THE FALL OF REBUS STATION

Rebus Station, Terra

"FALL BACK! Shira, blow the charges in three!" Critch shouted.

"Ready!" Shira yelled hoarsely. "Three…"

Critch grabbed Luther, pulled him to his feet, and slung the wounded man over his shoulder.

"Two…"

The three torrents—the only remaining uninjured from a team of ten—fell back from the scorched wall that separated them from the squads of dromadiers blasting relentlessly at the thick stone bricks outside. Smoke curled upward from small punctures created by relentless laser fire. The storage unit smelled of charred stone and disturbed dust, and the polluted hazy air etched at the torrents' throats, causing them to cough.

Critch, Dez, and Shira wore shemaghs over their noses and mouths, but breathing bad air for the past three hours was taking its toll. If they stayed there much longer, they'd suffocate, though the droms would blast through and cut them down long before that.

A blaster shot pierced the wall and into the ground near Critch's feet. He sidestepped as heat singed his toes through the leather boot.

"One…"

Critch ran toward the only door in the building. Luther groaned but remained otherwise limp.

"Boom!" Shira's yell was immediately echoed by a thunderous explosion a bare thirty feet in front of them.

The door exploded outward, away from them. Critch shielded his face, but heat and debris stung at his skin like wasps. If Shira had made the smallest error in setting the charge, the entire team would have been lying dead in pieces on the floor by now. Stings Critch could handle.

Daylight pierced the billowing smoke. He hustled toward it, carrying Luther, wishing for the strength and stamina he'd had during the Uprising twenty years earlier. Even though he was only in his forties, he felt twice his age from being chased nonstop. He'd kill for some stims. Hell, he'd kill for water.

Unencumbered, the other two members of Critch's team reached the doorway first and began shooting, finishing off any survivors from the squad that'd been guarding their only escape route. There was no bloodthirst in how Critch's team killed the droms—it was simply a matter of killing their enemy before their enemy killed them.

Critch jumped over a dead dromadier rather than weave around, even though the action made Luther feel twice as heavy on his shoulder. But he couldn't slow down. He knew they had only a few seconds before the squads on the other side of the building made their way around to finish off the ragged rebels.

He could already hear shouts in the distance, but he didn't look back. If the droms reached his team out in the open, there was nothing he could do. After two days of running, he no longer cared if he was shot in the chest or in the back. The way he saw it, either way he'd be dead.

Dez led them quickly to the much larger building next door. Shira leveled her rifle on the sidewalk behind Critch while he scrambled inside and out of the open daylight. She followed behind and closed the door. The sudden silence made Critch's panting sound all the louder.

Shira held out a hand. "Here, I can help carry him."

"No," Critch said. "I need you covering our six."

She didn't argue and aimed her rifle at the door.

Just because the droms couldn't see Critch's team didn't mean they couldn't find them. The droms had heat scanners, which they'd been using to peck away at Critch's team since they'd flushed the torrents out of the tunnels that crisscrossed the ground below Rebus Station.

"There's an access point in here," Dez said as he led Shira and Critch around pallets filled with boxes.

The door behind them slammed open, and an officer shouted commands as the sound of numerous boot steps entered the building. Dez cut around a row of crates. Critch found new strength in carrying Luther, and he could hear Shira at his back.

Critch noticed the *Faulk Industries* logo on one of the crates, which meant they likely held resources for Terra's fuel refineries. Somewhere in these crates would be enough explosives to finish off the droms chasing them. Too bad he wouldn't have the time to find them.

While Critch's team ran, the droms behind them moved cautiously, checking around each corner before putting themselves at risk. The droms had time on their side. With each day, more soldiers and more resources arrived. The CUF could hunt Critch until he collapsed, which was becoming more and more likely.

Luther's weight was taking its toll. Critch's legs burned.

Cramps in his right shoulder screamed at him. Sweat ran down his face, the scars causing it to run in jagged little streams rather than straight lines. He sucked in lungfuls of air untainted by blaster fire, but he still couldn't seem to take in enough oxygen. Luther had gone silent, likely passed out from his injuries, and Critch was thankful for that small mercy, knowing every movement must've been agony for his friend. The man had blaster shots through his gut and chest.

Critch desperately needed a reprieve, but the droms were relentless. A young soldier, not much more than a kid, had seen Critch in the tunnel a little over two days ago. Since then, the droms chasing them had only grown in numbers. There were plenty of other torrents on the lam throughout Rebus Station, but these squads would never divert from their current target. They had orders to chase him to the edges of the fringe if they had to.

Critch, whose real name was Drake Fender, was one of only two remaining torrent marshals leading the rebellion. The CUF would stop at nothing to see both Critch and Aramis Reyne dead, ideally at a public execution, which was the only reason Critch suspected the droms hadn't bombed the building they'd holed up in earlier that day.

Behind him, Critch could hear heavy boot steps as the soldiers fanned out to corner the torrents. Dez continued to lead the trio at a fast jog. When they reached the far wall, Dez checked the stacks of pallets, looking behind each. He stopped at one and pushed it to the side.

Critch was surprised to see the pallet move with ease, until he noticed it sat about a fraction of an inch off the ground, unlike the other pallets in the row. Someone had put wheels on the pallet and had done a good job at keeping them hidden.

Behind the pallet was a metal door with the words LANDQUAKE SHELTER stenciled above. Dez punched in a code on the wall keypad, and the heavy door whooshed open. Shira rushed through first, scanning the area with her rifle.

"Clear," she called out.

Critch had to duck to fit through with Luther, and he nearly stumbled down the steps beyond.

Behind him, Dez returned the pallet to its original place, then backed through and locked the door behind him. "Their heat sensors won't be able to scan through that. It ought to take them some time to find the door and break through, at least."

Critch let Luther down to the floor as gently as he could with his shaking, fatigued muscles. The man showed no sign of consciousness. In fact, he showed no sign of *anything*. Critch knelt and checked Luther's neck for a pulse. Nothing.

He'd been carrying a corpse.

"God damn it, Luther." He leaned back on his heels, his brows furrowed and his jaw tight. He took a deep breath. Luther had survived the Uprising, had survived the Citadel, and squeezed through some tight situations with Critch. He'd had a good run of luck.

The crap-thing about luck was that it could run out at any time.

Critch gave Luther a final touch on the shoulder. "May you find peace in the Eversea."

"May you find peace in the Eversea," Shira and Dez echoed behind him.

Critch removed the ammo from Luther's pockets and divided it among the three survivors. He pushed to his feet and reloaded his rifle, then checked his wrist comm. Still no response to his call for help. Not that he expected one after two days, but a small part of him still held hope that other teams had escaped. That Seda Faulk had not responded boded ill. Without Seda, the Fringe Liberation Campaign had no political face and minimal financial backing. In short, the fringe would be doomed.

He took a long breath before moving his gaze from his wrist comm to the surrounding room. His brows lifted when he realized they weren't in a landquake shelter after all. It was a tunnel, one Critch never even knew existed. He turned to Dez. "I take it you're familiar with this tunnel."

The young man nodded. "This is a private tube that connects all the Faulk Industries warehouses in this district. We used it to get to the different buildings faster."

"Where does it connect to a tunnel network?" Critch asked.

Dez shook his head. "It doesn't. This tunnel's a closed circuit, but I heard Seda had an artery built to the Third Street tunnels after Sol Base."

Critch grimaced. "The droms took Main; they might've taken Third Street by now. We'd do best to play hopscotch around the smaller tunnels until we can get clear of Rebus Station. Do you know if Seda built any shelters off this tube?"

Dez frowned. "Not that I know of." Then his eyes lit up. "But I know there's one in the Southtown tunnels. If we pop out at Warehouse Sixteen, it's just a couple blocks to Southtown."

Critch didn't tell Dez that two blocks inside a CUF-controlled city was two blocks farther than they could make without getting caught. Instead he said, "Lead me there."

"Want me to set a charge at the door, in case they break through?" Shira asked.

Critch turned to her. "How many charges do you have left?"

"One."

"No. Hold on to it. It could be our ace if we find ourselves in a hole."

Dez led the trio into the rough-cut tunnel. The kinetic lights with small gravity-powered spinners played dark shadow games in crevices. Rebus Station sat on a thick slab of sandstone. With good drilling equipment, it had been easy to build a labyrinth of tunnels below the city. The first tunnels had been built for workers to move through the city during the dust season, but the tunnels had proven to serve multiple uses. Twenty years ago, thousands of colonists survived the Uprising below ground when the CUF came down hard on protestors across the fringe. The CUF had not found the tunnels then. This time, they had.

It was only a matter of time before the CUF smoked out every last person in the tunnels. Many of those hiding below ground were not connected to the Fringe Liberation Campaign, but they'd be shown no mercy, their only fault not being born citizens.

Critch savored the cool quiet of the tunnel, though he knew the peace was temporary. If they didn't make it to a tunnel network by the time the droms broke through the door, this small, one-off passageway would become their last stand.

The somewhat-stale air became stifling with each passing minute that Critch didn't see an exit or branch. A straight tunnel meant an easy bottleneck. He worked his jaw to keep it from clenching. "Tell me this tunnel isn't just one long line."

"It's not... completely," Dez said with a hint of timidity before he skipped ahead. "See? Here's Warehouse Eight."

"Eight?" Shira asked. "You mean we still have eight blocks to go to get to Sixteen?"

Dez shrugged.

Critch scowled as he glanced first at the door and then down the long tunnel. "Pick up the pace, Dez."

Dez jogged. Critch's entire body felt like it could give out at any moment, but he managed to pick up his feet and keep pace with the younger man. Shira maintained a smooth pace behind Critch.

They crossed Warehouse Nine a few minutes later, and then Ten a few minutes after that.

When they reached Eleven, Dez slowed to take in the door standing wide open.

Critch pushed him forward. "Keep moving."

"But the door—" Dez began.

"This tunnel's been compromised," Critch said as a matter of fact, though he found himself raising his rifle a touch. "Keep your eyes on what's ahead."

They'd just passed Twelve when faint echoes of a distant explosion blew over them like a warm breeze.

"Shit," Dez muttered and sped up.

In a straight tunnel, the droms had the advantage. They were fresh and could run faster. They had blasters and could rain laser fire through the tunnel from the entrance and hit the torrents. Sure, the torrents had rifles and could shoot back, but that'd be a waste of ammo. Critch carried a photon handgun, but it would do little in a gunfight against a squad carrying battle blasters.

Critch counted on the droms not shooting blind in their quest to catch him alive. He ran forward and didn't look back. His breaths came hard, and he stumbled somewhere between Thirteen and Fourteen. Shira helped him to his feet, though she was breathing as heavily as Critch. Dez continued to sprint ahead with his rifle raised.

Dez ran past Fifteen, but Critch stopped, Shira halting at his side. Someone, covered by a dirt-brown blanket, huddled by the stairs. Critch approached, his finger on the trigger. The shape moved, and he realized the figure was a woman holding a toddler. When her gaze fell upon his face, her eyes widened. "Marshal Fender?"

"Droms are coming," Critch croaked. He motioned to the top of the stairs. "Can you open that door?"

She gave a small nod.

"Good. Get out of here."

He didn't wait to see if she obeyed. He turned and ran. He saw Dez stop ahead and look back. "Sixteen! We made it!"

Dez ran up the stairs and opened the door. Blaster shots

rained in from the other side, and Dez tumbled back down the stairs and onto the tunnel floor, his body blackened and bloody from at least a dozen kill-shots. As Dez fell, Critch halted, spun around, and nearly tumbled over Shira, who was slower to react to the new danger.

"Move!" Critch pressed her back the way they'd come, and the pair raced away from their fallen comrade. By the time they reached Fifteen, the colonist was no longer in sight and the door was closing. Critch lunged up the stairs and pushed the door open, throwing the woman back.

"Droms are here. Hide!" Critch yelled, slamming the door closed the instant Shira was through.

The woman, clutching her wide-eyed toddler in her arms, spun in a frantic rush before running off to the right, down a row of crates on pallets. Critch ran left in an attempt to keep the droms off her. Shira stayed glued behind him, covering his back, even though she could outrun him. This warehouse, much like the first one they'd run through, was filled with rows of stacked, loaded pallets. Rather than weaving, Critch ran straight down the main aisle to put distance between themselves and their enemy.

When they were halfway through the building, an explosion behind signaled the tunnel door was wide open and droms would be pouring in. After being on the lam nonstop, Critch no longer acknowledged the fear of being caught. What he did fear was the dullness creeping through his veins like gelled diesel fuel, suffocating his remaining strength. Running without food and not nearly enough water was weakening him. Each of his boots felt like it weighed a ton, and it was becoming a feat to keep from stumbling. If he fell now, he wasn't sure he could get back up.

The sound of a woman's plea, shots, and silence caused Critch to look over his shoulder and beyond Shira. Anger singed his heart. That pair of colonists would've posed no risk to the armed soldiers. Yet, they'd been gunned down.

Critch used his fury as fuel to drive him forward. The building's main doors ominously stood at the end of the center aisle. He needed to go through them to reach the next tunnels, but how many dromadiers waited outside?

When he reached the doors, he took a sharp left and ran toward the stairs, with Shira staying right behind him. They were both Terrans—they thrived in the tunnels; they never sought higher ground. Still, they continued.

"Stop, or we'll shoot!" someone shouted.

Neither stopped, and Shira reached the stairs as quickly as he did. Critch grabbed the handrail for support as he took the steps two at a time. They panted as they climbed. Sweat burned his eyes. He could hear the droms reach the steps and quickly close the distance.

Critch and Shira made it to the second floor, and Critch reached out for the door. Blaster shots hit the surrounding wall. Shira cried out. Critch snapped around as she fell back, tumbling down the stairs until her momentum was stopped by a dromadier who had four compatriots at his back.

One of the droms knocked Shira's rifle away, even though the shot through her chest made it pretty clear she had only moments of life remaining.

"Stop, Fender, or we will shoot you!" the lead dromadier ordered.

"Screw that. He killed Benson." The twitchy drom closest to Shira raised his blaster even higher.

"Don't kill him, Hills. That's an order!" the leader said.

Critch first eyed Twitchy to make sure he'd obey his commander, then spared a glance at Shira to find her watching him. She looked at her hand quickly, and he noticed she held the explosive charge. Her expression, wracked with pain, spoke of resolve. He hoped she'd seen the respect he had for her in his own expression.

"Drop your rifle, Fender," the leader said. "You're under arrest for bioterrorism and the murder of over six hundred citizens."

He swallowed. His rifle dropped to the floor with a solid *thunk* of metal hitting tile. He turned his eyes to Twitchy, who was clearly on the edge of disobeying orders. Critch's lip curved upward. Twitchy's eyes narrowed, and he aimed his rifle.

The explosion engulfed Twitchy before it swallowed the half-squad. Critch lunged for the door handle, but the shockwave hit him before he could grab it. He smashed into the wall. Fire and agony came next. The blast dissipated, and he took a labored breath. Every rib was a sword against his lungs, and he groaned his exhalation.

The deafening ringing in his ears was the only sound he could hear, and his eyes opened to reveal a world in vertigo. He clenched his eyes closed until he had forced several more breaths. When he opened them again, the world still spun, but he could make out snapshots: an open space where the stairs had stood, millions of dust motes in the air, no sign of anyone—dead or alive.

He moaned again when he tried to push himself to his hands and knees, only to collapse. He felt himself being pulled up. He tried to look, but the movement caused his vision to swirl. All he could do was fight to retain consciousness as he was dragged away. His consciousness soon faded to numbness.

Critch awoke to find himself on his back in a place he didn't recognize. A subdued voice was speaking in the background. He held back his inclination to move in order to get his bearings. His body felt like he was on a planet with a gravity of at least 3g. His ribs protested with every breath, but they gave dull aches rather than sharp stabs, which meant none were broken. Much of his body throbbed, but his left shoulder bore a familiar pain. *Not again.* He squeezed his left fist, and his shoulder burned. Yeah, the damn joint had been thrown out again. At least it had been reset, so he didn't have to deal with that experience. Still, his arm would be useless until he got meds and tape.

He stared at the cracked white ceiling above him until the room quit spinning. Pieces of the paint were missing, either from disrepair or from the recent bombings. Without moving his head, he scanned as much of the room he could. It was tiny—likely an apartment—with a kitchenette off to the side of the living room where he lay. A small wall-screen was playing the news, which explained the voice he'd heard.

Unless the CUF had taken him to someone's home, he was most definitely not in the hands of the dromadiers.

Using his right arm to brace himself, Critch tried to push himself up, but his body refused to move. He glared at the ceiling. "Fuck me."

"Be careful, Marshal. You're lucky to be alive."

Startled, Critch turned toward the voice to see a young man approach. No more than sixteen and dressed in the baggy brown canvas coveralls worn by nearly all Rebus Station workers.

"Where am I?" Critch asked, wishing he could sit up.

"You're in my apartment. Well, it's my family's apartment, technically. I'm Kassel."

"How'd I get here?"

"I found you. My friends and I were scavenging through the warehouses when the droms showed up. We were hiding on the second floor and then there was this huge explosion. We went to take the stairs to leave, but they were gone, and you were there. We saw more droms coming down the street, so we grabbed you and brought you here."

"You shouldn't have taken me," Critch said. "They'll shoot you for helping me."

Kassel shrugged. "They'd shoot me anyway, just because they can. They've been treating Rebus Station like a shooting range ever since you blew that destroyer." He walked over to the wall-screen and turned up the volume. "It's been all over the news."

Parliament had proven time and again that the citizens had no interest in treating the colonies as equals, even though most of the Collective's resources came from the fringe. When Seda had negotiated the cease-fire, Critch had let himself believe there was hope without war. Parliament had wasted little time in proving him wrong.

He scowled and turned to the screen. A reporter was standing outside the Parliament building on Myr.

"As of ten o'clock Myrad sol time, Parliament declared war after this week's slaughter of five citizens on Terra. We are now in a civil war between the Collective's foundational worlds—Alluvia and Myr—and its colony planets—Terra, Darios, Spate, and Playa. The Collective Unified Forces, now under command of Corps General Maximus Laciam, has taken control of Rebus Station on Terra, and we expect to have control of Devil Town on Spate this week. Sol Base of Darios remains under CUF control. As you may remember, Ice Port of Playa was bombed last year in retaliation for bioterrorism and is no longer in operation. Once the CUF has secured control of the remaining fringe station, all other colonies on each planet are expected to submit with minimal resistance. Senator Gabriel Heid, the co-chair of Parliament, is pushing for a fast resolution to minimize impacts to our daily lives. To support the CUF, Parliament has initiated the draft on Myr and Alluvia, and has extended service indefinitely on all colonist conscripts currently serving the CUF. Senator Heid has requested that all citizens remain calm, as Alluvia and Myr are protected from attack. This broadcast will repeat every thirty minutes or as new updates arrive. I'm Willas James with DZ-Five News. Stay safe, stay united."

Critch's jaw tightened more and more while the broadcast replayed. He knew of only two Heids. Gabriela Heid was dead. That left the other Heid. Gabriel Heid, leader of the clandestine Founders, murderer of his own daughter, and number one on Critch's kill-list.

"See?" Kassel said. "Us colonists mean nothing to them. We're disposable."

"The idiots never learned they need us to survive, not the other way around. But they'll learn soon enough."

Kassel balked. "You saw the news. They've already taken Rebus Station, which means they have control of the space docks. All the other Terran colonies will fall without any kind of space support."

"If they fall, it'll be temporary. Heid was wrong about one thing. Alluvia and Myr aren't safe," Critch said. Using every ounce of energy and too much exertion, he pushed himself up into a seated position. "Because I'm taking the war to them."

CHAPTER 4

GHOST TOWN

Sol Base, Darios

"THIS IS CREEPY," Sixx said.

"You won't hear me tell you differently," Reyne said as they passed an empty food cart in Sol Base.

"The last time I was here," Sixx continued, "the street was so crowded, I couldn't even see who grabbed my ass."

"Don't you mean who tried to pickpocket you?"

"Same difference."

The pair strolled down Main Street. What was once Darios's largest colony, and home to the busiest fringe station, was now practically a ghost town. The blight had cleared out the entire population. After Reyne had sprayed fungicide over the colony, eradicating the deadly blight, the CUF had wasted no time in securing the fringe station and its space docks.

With the CUF fully in control, few colonists had any interest in settling the colony. The planet produced a huge portion of the Collective's food supply, including all the philoseed and cavote, two bean-like staples in every civilian and colonist's diet. Alluvia and Myr depended on Darios, making Sol Base the CUF's most closely-guarded colony. Darios's value to the Collective also meant it was the most highly regulated, with over eighty percent tariffs on all exports.

It had taken offers of free housing and guaranteed income to draw in even the minimum few hundred colonists required to get the fringe station and its space docks back up and running. Before the blight, Sol Base was the home to over seventy thousand colonists. Now, all the dromadiers, traders, and colonists totaled less than one percent of pre-blight numbers.

Anything the blight had touched had to be decontaminated. A massive hole, a mile in diameter, was dug to burn and then bury all the bodies in. Bulldozers and trucks ran nonstop for over a month cleaning out the colony. It took contractors another three months to sanitize the buildings and streets. Now, everything glistened like new construction.

Reyne looked to the horizon, where the mass grave stood—a hill covered in new prairie grasses. There were no signs, no structures to memorialize the area. That would cost money, and Parliament never saw fit to spend money on the fringe if it didn't net a return. Parliament should've not only built a memorial but also paid a token to the relatives of those killed. After all, it was Senator Gabriel Heid who'd been responsible for dropping the blight on Sol Base. Heid had never claimed credit for the massacre; hell, he'd even spun the story and put the blame on the torrents. The puppet master was behind every major event that had taken place in the Collective over the past few years, and Reyne would see that he was stopped.

Reyne scowled and turned away from the mass grave.

"A lot of good people died that day," Sixx said.

Reyne noticed his friend had been watching him. "You mean folks like Double-jointed Sally?"

Sixx shook his head. "She was talented, but she wasn't good. That woman beat on kids. No, I'm thinking of folks like Lamitie."

"The constable who arrested you for theft?"

Sixx shrugged. "It was my fault I got caught. Lamitie—he was one of the good ones. He was always looking out for those who needed looking out for."

"Yeah. I remember," Reyne agreed as images of other Sol Base residents passed through his mind. Some he'd met once, some he'd known for decades, and some he wished he'd had the chance to meet. All of their deaths were a part of a political ploy to bring public opinion down on the fringe. "They're the reason why we fight: to stop the Collective from doing things like this again."

"Preaching to the choir, boss."

Reyne chuckled. "Like you've ever been to church."

"I have. Once. I'll tell you about it sometime."

Sixx pinched the brim of his hat as they met a pair of dromadiers coming from the other direction. "Ladies," he said.

They continued without sparing a glance to either Sixx or Reyne.

"Careful," Reyne cautioned.

"Always am," Sixx replied. "Those two were clearly colonist conscripts. If they recognized us, they'd just as likely let us pass. But right now, even our own mothers wouldn't recognize us."

They each wore the full beards commonly worn by Darion men. Sunglasses and hats also helped hide their features while blending them in perfectly as Darions.

"All it takes is a single drom to report us and we're busted," Reyne said. "Plus, there are so few colonists in Sol Base, the droms might recognize any newcomers."

"When did you get all unadventurous?" Sixx asked.

"Since my profile topped the CUF's Most Wanted list."

"I think Critch may still be one above you. Taking out that destroyer this week amped up his notoriety a few notches."

"He can keep it." Reyne stopped, turned, and looked at the business front before them. "We're here."

He led Sixx into the tourist shop. The shop was empty of tourists, and only a single cashier stood at the far end. She was young, barely a teenager, and didn't look up from her comm screen. The two men strolled down the center aisle, which was lined with snacks containing philoseed or cavote, some using the staples in rather creative ways. Reyne paused every few steps to check out the merchandise.

"Pickled philo is surprisingly tasty," Sixx said.

Reyne wrinkled his nose and continued without comment. Near the back of the store, he found a bin of multipurpose tools. He rummaged through and pulled out a tool with a rainbow-colored handle. He brought it over to the counter and set it down. The cashier glanced up only to scan the tool.

Sixx dropped two shirts on the counter.

Reyne lifted the clothing. "What's this?"

"I promised Lily I'd pick up a souvenir for her from every colony I visit."

"And the other?"

Sixx shrugged. "I think Bree would like it."

Reyne let out a sigh, even though he inwardly gave Sixx kudos for thinking of his daughter-of-sorts and their newest crew member. He motioned to the cashier to scan the items, then held up his wrist comm for payment. After he paid, Reyne grabbed the tool and tossed the two shirts at Sixx.

"You should see our newest inventory; they're nesting dolls. Each one's hand-painted." The girl pointed to a wall display without looking up from her wrist comm.

"Oh. Okay." Reyne walked over to the display and casually examined one of the dolls. He set it back down after a minute. He looked around, but there were still only the three of them in the store. Their contact should've been there by now. He took another look at the tool. He'd chosen the right one. The message had said to buy a rainbow-colored tool for the all-clear sign and a red-handled tool if they'd been followed. Reyne may be old, but his memory was still sharp as ever.

"Lily might like one of these dolls," Sixx said as he opened one.

Reyne frowned. "Lily? She's obsessed with everything tech. She'd hate these. You should get her a tablet."

"Vym's already got her one," Sixx said. "She's basically adopted Lily as her granddaughter."

Before Reyne could respond, a man walked into the store. "Bob? Is that you?"

Reyne smiled and headed over to the newcomer. "Buddy! It's been ages."

The man closed the distance. "I thought it was you through the window, so I stopped in to see."

They embraced. When they stepped back, Sixx came to stand next to Reyne.

The other man spoke first. "How's your family?"

"Everyone's good. Yours?"

"Good. Kathy's pregnant again. That'll be number three for us."

"Congratulations," Reyne said.

"Crops looking good this season?"

"As good as can be expected," Reyne said. "Yours?"

"Same." The man looked around. "Well, I guess I'd better get back to it. You take care."

"You, too." Reyne shook the man's hand.

The man departed. Reyne and Sixx left the store and went back onto Main Street.

"You ever see that guy before?" Sixx asked quietly.

"Nope," Reyne replied. He stuck his hands in his pockets as they continued their walk down Main Street. His fingers in his left pocket brushed against a metal key, a key that hadn't been there before. He gripped the key as they walked three more blocks until they reached the housing complex.

The complex, known as the Villages, consisted of eight buildings Parliament had allocated to new Sol Base colonists. They weren't the worst condominiums in town, but they were nowhere near the most luxurious. *Parliament always has to show the fringe where they stand in the big picture.*

What the complex lacked in amenities, it made up for in its autonomy. The CUF, believing it had Sol Base locked down tight, had turned over security to local constabulary forces while the droms remained focused on the station and its docks. Reyne couldn't see a single dromadier within the entire block. If everything went as planned, that decision would prove to be a very bad mistake for the CUF stationed on Darios.

Unknown to the CUF, Sol Base was about to become the tip of the torrent spear in the fight for freedom.

Reyne headed to the second building on his right. Above the door hung a sign that read Harvest View–Building 3. The pair entered and took the stairs up to the third floor. Like the rest of Sol Base, this building smelled of disinfectant. They came across no one as they walked down the hallway, even though it was in the middle of the workday.

"Quite the bustling community," Sixx said as he stayed close to Reyne's side, his hand near his waist, where Reyne knew Sixx had a blaster holstered.

Reyne stopped when they reached a door with the number 3-35 imprinted on the metal. Reyne pulled out the key, confirmed the number on the key, and unlocked the door.

Sixx entered first, pulling out his blaster the moment he was through. "We got company, boss."

Reyne stepped in and found an attractive woman lounging in a chair, a guard standing on each side. "It's okay, Sixx. You can lower your weapon," Reyne said without taking his eyes off the woman. "It's good to see you, Hatha."

She smiled and motioned for Reyne to take a seat. "Aramis, it's been far too long."

Reyne took a seat, thankful to rest his arthritic joints, while Sixx remained in a guard position at his back. "I've been a bit busy."

Her brow rose. "Just a bit? Between helping out refugees and recruiting for the war, I'm surprised you could fit in time to see me." She gave a knowing smile. "But then, that's why you're here, isn't it? So, which of those two things do you need my help with?"

"Both," Reyne replied quickly. "And from what I hear along the space-line, you're already deep into both refugees and freedom fighting."

She sobered. "That awful blight wiped out my beautiful city, along with my husband and three children. We all know it was created by citizens and delivered by citizens. Who could blame me for wanting anyone associated with Alluvia or Myr off my planet?"

"I certainly wouldn't blame you."

Her gaze wandered as sad memories seemed to take her to another place. After a moment, she took in a breath. "I'm short on time today. Tell me what you need, and let's see what we can do for each other."

Reyne leaned forward. "I'll lay all my cards on the table. I need you, Hatha. The Darion resistance reports to you. Every colonist on this world respects you and would do anything you ask. I know you're planning to take over Sol Base, and I'm here to offer up as many resources as I can muster to help you accomplish that."

She leaned forward. "I thought the torrents were split across all the other fringe worlds."

"They are," Reyne said. "But I've been talking with Seda Faulk and Vym Patel. We believe that if we can take and retain Darios, the Collective will be forced to negotiate."

"Or else they'll starve," she said.

"Or else they'll starve," he echoed.

She steepled her hands. "Exactly what kind of resources are we looking at?"

"We've been printing munitions nonstop for over a year. We also have roughly twelve thousand torrents on Spate and Playa who we can begin transporting to the dock you've been building near Thunder Canyon."

"Not my dock. Over a thousand Darions have been working full time—with no salary—building that dock. It's *their* dock, and they're calling it New Sol. It's nearly complete, but don't get your hopes up. Without access to Collective technology for the systems and launchpads, all we could build was a single slingshot dock. The largest ship that could be launched there is a class G."

Reyne frowned. "That's slows things down a couple of weeks, but if we get started now, we could get all the torrents down here within a month. That's assuming you can keep the dock hidden from CUF scanners."

"Don't worry about me. Worry about how your transports will come in without raising suspicion. In case you didn't notice, there's a shiny warship with a full complement sitting above Sol Base."

Reyne smiled. "Yes. Sitting above Sol Base. In the past week, there hasn't been a patrol ship sent more than five hundred miles out from here. When you withdrew your fighters from the city's edges, the droms suddenly felt a lot more comfortable around here."

She rolled her eyes. "They think they scared off the resistance. They're so prideful, they've never thought to consider the resistance has the upper hand here. Already, the resistance within this city outnumbers dromadiers nearly six to one."

"Taking Sol Base from the ground doesn't worry me nearly as much as how we're going to deal with the warship parked overhead."

"I don't suppose you have any more of that blight on hand?"

Reyne's jaw tightened. "No. Even if I did, I can guarantee I'd burn it the first chance I had."

She sighed. "Then, no, I don't have a plan yet for dealing with those ships up there. I welcome any suggestions."

"Vym has analysts working on scenarios. When we have options, I'll be sure to get them to you."

"Fair enough." She leaned back in her chair. "I hope you realize that evicting the CUF from Sol Base will be far easier than keeping them from returning. Darios provides over seventy percent of the Collective's food. When Sol Base was hit, losing a season of food dropped the Collective into a severe recession. Imagine what will happen if we intentionally cut off the food supply. Parliament will send in every dromadier they have to reclaim Sol Base. It could open up the chance for them to change us from tenured workers to slaves, which I suspect they'd prefer."

"That's why I'm not asking you to cut off the food supplies," Reyne said. "I know Darions rely on Myr and Alluvia as much as Myr and Alluvia rely on you. Even with the ludicrous tariffs, they're your biggest income sources."

She thought for a moment, and her lips curved upward. "They are; however, I suppose there are some things I can do to help inspire negotiations to end the war and lead to the independence of every Darion. Darios will be free."

"The fringe will be free," Reyne said.

Hatha stood.

"There's one more thing," Reyne said, coming to his feet.

"We're taking on hundreds of new mouths to feed every day."

She smiled. "And Darios has plenty of food."

He nodded.

"I'll run the numbers. I'll divert as much as I can without raising suspicion. We can load the transports when they begin to arrive." She glanced out the window. "We can make this work as long as the CUF believes it controls Sol Base and, therefore, all of Darios. If it gets even a twitch of suspicion, we'll see the entire armada in orbit within a week. If the CUF controls the space above us, it quite effectively cuts off our wings."

"I understand," Reyne said. "We'll do what it takes to see Sol Base in your hands. The CUF thinks there's nothing left worth taking on Playa, so it's left only a single destroyer in orbit. Vym can load and send transports out from there as fast as they can come."

"Speaking of Vym, I hear she has five Andre printers running now."

"One Andre. Four slightly smaller Andre-generics printed off the first printer."

"I want one."

Reyne's lips thinned. The 3D printers, especially the largest Andre printers, were the most valuable asset anyone could have. To get their hands on one was the reason they'd gone after a CUF supply ship. It was a game-changer. "I'll see what I can do," he said finally.

She smiled and nodded to one of her guards, who handed her a tablet, and she in turn handed it to Reyne. "This is an encrypted tablet. Use this for communications going forward. Also, this room is yours for as long as you need. You can always find sanctuary here."

"Much obliged."

"Tell Seda he continues to have my full support in his representing the colonies."

Reyne gave a small nod, and she exited along with her two guards.

Reyne reclaimed his chair, examined the tablet, and set it on the table.

Sixx checked the locks before walking over to Reyne and taking a nearby seat. "Well, that was easier than I thought it'd be."

"I wasn't worried about getting her support," Reyne said. "I'm more worried she's going to take our army to run her own war against the Collective."

"Is that a bad thing?"

"It can be if she only cares about gaining independence for Darios and leaves the rest of the fringe at the mercy of Heid and his crony senators in Parliament."

Sixx thought for a moment before speaking. "Worst-case scenario: even if only Darios broke free, it would set a precedent for the other colonies. You said yourself that Darios is the key. As long as it breaks free, there's hope for the fringe."

"Darios has always been the key. I think Heid had the blight dropped on Sol Base to ensure the city was under CUF control before things had a chance to get out of hand."

Sixx chuckled drily. "Yeah, and only kill seventy thousand colonists at the same time."

"Seventy thousand potential torrents," Reyne corrected. "Heid thought he had everything planned with his fellow Founders. He tried to have Vym killed, and never counted on Seda breaking faith. If it weren't for those two helping the cause, we'd still be small, harmless clusters of resistance fighters."

Sixx grinned. "I hope I'm there to see the look on that man's face when we take Sol Base."

Reyne sat and thought through all the plots Heid had hatched over the past decade to hold the Collective together. Even now, Reyne wondered if Heid wasn't still one step ahead of them. He sighed. "I hope so, too."

CHAPTER 5

THE BITTERS OF WAR

Rebus Station, Terra

CRITCH HAD JUST OPENED the door when Kassel jogged out from his bedroom. "Wait! I'm coming with you."

"No, you're not," Critch said.

"Yes, I am."

Critch sighed, closed the door, and turned to face the teenager. Kassel watched him intently while he tried to zip shut an overstuffed backpack.

"Listen, kid. I've stayed here too long already. Every minute I stay here, I put you and your family in more danger. The droms will come looking for me. You're a lot safer if I'm not here."

Kassel shrugged. "No one's safe around here anymore. I want to go with you. I want to fight."

"You're too young."

"You were only two years older than me when you fought in the Uprising."

Critch pursed his lips before he spoke again. "I'm not going to let you get yourself killed."

"I can take care of myself. Besides, I remember that *you* almost got yourself killed, and it was *me* who dragged your unconscious ass to safety."

He sighed. "This matter is not up for debate. You're staying. Your parents will go nuts when they come home and you're not here."

Kassel's eyes narrowed, and his jaw jutted out. "My parents aren't coming back. They were caught after curfew last week."

Critch paused as he watched the teenager. Kassel's jaw trembled as though he was about to cry, but he stood tall. If his parents were caught after curfew, they were dead. The CUF made no exceptions. Not anymore.

Kassel finished zipping his backpack and slung it over his shoulders. The pair stood in a face-off.

The last thing Critch wanted was to bring kids into war, but the truth was, war had already come to them. There was no escape from the violence. Kassel was still at the age of invincibility—he could take on the galaxy and still make it home for dinner. At least Critch could keep an eye on Kassel if he took the kid with him, whereas if Kassel stayed behind, Critch couldn't keep him from going after the droms on his own.

He let out a deep breath. "Okay, kid."

Kassel's features brightened as he broke out into a full grin.

"But, you do as I say, no exception, no argument. Got it?"

His head bobbed up and down. "Got it."

Critch nodded to the boy's pack. "Let me see what you packed."

Kassel hurriedly shrugged off the backpack and handed it over.

Critch unzipped the bag and dumped the contents on the nearby table. Clothes, toiletries, books, and various trinkets tumbled out. He picked out a toy spaceship and held it up with his brow raised in an unasked question.

"Dad gave me that," Kassel defended. "I'm going to be a pilot."

Critch set the ship on the pile. "We're running for our lives; we're not camping out. Take only what you need to survive. That means this bag should be filled with food and water." He rifled through the contents and pulled out a small first aid kit. "This is smart. Keep the kit. If you have a knife, take it. And grab some gloves and a shemagh—you'll need them."

"What's a shem—"

"A bandana or a scarf. Something to cover your face. Where we're headed, you'll need it."

"Where are we headed?"

"Broken Mountain."

Kassel's jaw slackened. "But that place is—it—"

"I know. That's why droms avoid it, and that's why we're headed there. Now, get your pack ready and let's go."

Kassel swooped up the bag and its contents in his arms and hustled toward his room before pausing. He turned. "You better not leave me."

"I won't. You're one of mine now."

Kassel beamed and disappeared into his room, and a flurry of rummaging sounds followed.

Critch turned his attention to the dinette. He unslung his pack, favoring his weak shoulder. He took a chair—his body still ached with battle fatigue—and set his full pack next to him.

A few minutes later, Kassel emerged with a much emptier bag.

"Now, fill the rest with food and water, especially water," Critch ordered before looking down at his wrist comm. Still no response from Seda. Ditto from Gabe on the *Honorless*. Seda was understandable—Critch had known Seda would have to go dark after fleeing Terra. Gabe, on the other hand, was supposed to be parked behind one of Terra's twin moons, waiting specifically for

Critch's call. That Gabe hadn't answered meant one of three things: either the CUF had managed to block all comms leaving Terra, the *Honorless* had been taken or destroyed, or Gabe had abandoned Critch and the rest of the crew.

For Gabe's sake, it'd better be one of the first two options. Frustrated, he tapped a quick message to Birk on the *Scorpia*.

RS gone to shit. Need a ride with stealth. RP at BM.

The last intel Critch had on his friend was that Birk and Throttle were on their way to Spate to raise a ruckus with the droms in Devil Town. While the "Devil's Playground" mission was more important than rescuing Critch, he hoped Birk could track down one of the specters—his pirate fleet turned torrent fleet—to make a pickup. With their stealth capability, they could bypass the shitstorm above Rebus Station.

As for the rest of Critch's crew, they'd separated a week ago to hunt down supplies. He'd yet to hear from them and suspected the worst. He put his wrist comm back into standby mode to keep any sniffer drones from picking up a signal, even though drones couldn't pick up a signal unless they were within a dozen feet of it.

"Can I get one of those?" Kassel asked.

Critch looked up to see the boy eyeing his wrist comm. "We get off this rock, I'll get you a top-of-the-line comm."

"Cool."

Critch pointed to the window. "Curfew's in three hours. We need to make it to the tunnels by then."

Kassel's eyes widened. "The nearest tunnel is eight blocks from here."

"But you were in the warehouse district." Critch frowned. "Exactly how did you get me back to your place without getting stopped by droms?"

"It was easy. I drove my parents' truck. Arick and Jams distracted the droms while I wheeled you out in a crate and loaded you into the back of the truck. A couple droms saw me, but they don't seem to bother with the looters right now." He nodded to the torrent pendant Critch wore. "They're too focused on finding folks wearing the teardrops. Do I get one of those?"

"Maybe later. Tell me about the checkpoints around here."

"Sure," the boy said. "It's easy enough leaving town. Conscripts operate those checkpoints, and they don't care—I think they want people to get out of this shithole. It's getting back into town that's the hard part. All the droms are citizens at the entry checkpoints, and they're assholes."

"When we come back, we won't care, because we'll bring an army of vengeance with us."

"Cool," Kassel said again, this time with much more hope.

"Let's head out," Critch said.

Critch covered his scarred face with his shemagh, and they left Kassel's apartment building. They ran across other Terrans in the hallway. All gave Critch sharp looks, but they continued along their way after seeing Kassel was both unharmed and clearly not a prisoner.

The truck was parked across the street, and the pair jogged over and climbed in. Critch let Kassel drive, since it was his parents' vehicle and he knew the checkpoints. More important, with the teen behind the wheel, Critch had his hands free to shoot if things turned dire.

"Let's hope you fly better than you drive," Critch said after Kassel overcorrected the wheel and abruptly hit the brake, then the gas pedal, all within a couple of seconds.

"I don't know how to fly yet. Wait, does that mean you'll teach me?" His voice climbed in pitch as he asked.

"One thing at a time, kid. Focus on your driving first. I'd rather die fighting than pancaked into the side of a building."

Kassel's driving didn't improve, but they passed through the residential neighborhood rather quickly. Critch was surprised to see few dromadiers walking the sidewalks or driving patrols until he realized the CUF would be focusing its numbers on chasing down torrents. The CUF had the ships and weapons, but the fringe had the numbers. The CUF could win a short war if it hit hard and fast. But, if the torrents could prolong the war using guerilla-style attacks, forcing the Collective to burn through its resources, the fringe had the upper hand.

While he didn't crave a long war, he'd do whatever it took to free the colonies, even if it meant he'd be fighting the rest of his life.

Flashing lights caught his attention, and he saw a pair of droms standing at a checkpoint. "Okay," Critch began, "This is how this is going to play out. We're driving to my sister's place in Hampton. I've been working all day and sleeping. Anything goes sideways, I'll take out the droms and you step on it. Got it?"

"Got it," Kassel said before he squinted at the two droms. He grinned. "We won't need a story. May and Leony are working. They're both conscripts—from Spate, I think—and they *hate* the CUF."

"Even if that's true, they can't see my face," Critch cautioned. "If they knowingly let me pass, it's a death sentence for them."

"Oh. Then you'd better keep your face covered."

"Good plan," Critch said drily. He lowered his head against the window and closed his eyes, allowing the barest of slits to see through. At the same time, he pulled out his blaster and held it against his waist, aimed at Kassel's open window.

The truck slowed as they approached the two dromadiers. Conscripts wore the same dark blue suits as citizens, except their uniforms were missing either the Myrad or Alluvian flag patches worn by citizens. And no conscripts could become officers.

Kassel hung his arm out his window. "Hey, ladies. How are you doing on this lovely Thursday?"

One of the droms stepped forward. She looked into the truck. "Where's your pals?"

"Family trip today, Leony," Kassel said. "My dad and I are heading out to my aunt's in Hampton. She busted her leg today."

"Yeah, yeah, whatever. You know the rules. I've got to log everyone who passes through here."

Critch's grip around the blaster tightened.

"I remember the rules, sure, but everyone knows that being on the lists is no good. And I know how busy you are. You probably don't even get time for breaks. You know, if your mouth is feeling a bit dry, I might have something to quench your thirst."

"It'd better be none of that watered-down crap you gave me last time."

"Nope. It's a brand-new bottle of Double-Moon to quench your thirst."

The woman lifted her nose. "Prove it."

Kassel reached under his seat and pulled out a bottle of Terran whiskey Critch hadn't known was there. The kid handed it to the woman.

She looked at it for a moment before unscrewing the cap and taking a drink. Her eyes squeezed shut. "Oh, yeah, that's the real stuff right there."

"How about one for me?" the other woman asked as she approached the truck.

Critch tensed even more.

Kassel's face fell. "Sorry, May. I've only got the one this time, but I promise I'll bring you one next time."

"Anyone who says, 'next time' never plans on coming through here again. You said yourself you're heading to your aunt's. I'd bet you're heading out for good. Is that what you're doing?"

"Nope," Kassel said a bit too quickly.

"How about your pops?" she asked.

"He's sleeping," Kassel said.

"Sure, he is." She slapped the windshield. "Wakey, wakey."

Critch slowly opened his eyes all the way.

Both women watched him, even though the one seemed far more interested in her new bottle of whiskey.

"Come on, May. Dad's had a long day. He's beat."

"He can speak for himself," May said. "How about it, Daddy? You got an extra bottle of Double-Moon for me?"

"Sorry, pal," Critch said, keeping the hidden blaster leveled on her. "Whiskey's getting hard to come by."

She squinted. "Wait. Let me see your face."

Critch watched her for a long moment. When she didn't break eye contact, he took his free hand and tugged down his shemagh. At the same time, he raised the blaster to a better position to make a clear shot.

Recognition filled May's features.

Ah, hell, Critch thought as he got ready to pull the trigger.

"You're him," she said. Her compatriot took a step forward as well, lowering the bottle, as she stared.

Neither woman seemed to notice or care that Critch held the blaster at them. He said nothing. If they'd been citizens, he would've killed them already. Conscripts were another story. Parliament had instituted a required two-year service for all able bodied and able-minded colonists upon reaching the age of eighteen. It was Parliament's attempt at indoctrinating colonists into the Collective's ideals, but since many conscripts were treated like indentured servants, required service instead wedged a wider divide between citizens and the fringe; especially since citizens had no service requirement.

"We don't want any trouble," Kassel said. "We just want to be on our way."

"My dad fought under you in the Uprising," Leony said.

"What's his name?" Critch asked.

"Leon Brahams," she replied.

Critch thought for a moment. "I remember Leon. He was one of the best roosters around. He carried the heavy stuff and could open hell on the blue bastards." He paused. "Leon was Terran. Aren't you Spaten?"

A prideful smile grew on Leony's face as Critch spoke of her father. "He came to Spate after the Uprising. That's where he met my mom. She convinced him to stay, and the rest is history."

"Until you were conscripted at eighteen and ended up on your father's homeland," Critch said.

Leony sobered. "Yeah, well there's nothing I can do about it. They kill deserters."

"There's always something someone can do if it's important enough," he countered. "Conscripts outnumber citizens in the dromadier squads. Imagine what could change if the conscripts all rose up as one force. Or, imagine what each conscript could do if she put her mind to it. Just letting torrents and refugees through your checkpoint can save many lives."

"Helping colonists is one thing, but we'd be killed if they found out we knowingly helped torrents," May countered.

"True. It all comes down to if the something that needs done is important enough," Critch said. "What do you think?"

May and Leony looked at each other and then at Critch.

May spoke. "You can go. We won't tell anyone."

Leony tried to hand the bottle of whiskey back to Kassel.

"Keep it," Critch said. "You're doing a good thing here."

Critch nodded at Kassel, and they drove through the checkpoint and left Rebus Station. With dusk came the reddish glow of the two moons that illuminated Terra's nights. They drove for miles without speaking. Kassel was the first to break the silence.

"How many more torrents do you think are still stuck in Rebus Station?" the boy asked.

"Too many," Critch said. "Several hundred, at least."

More silence.

Several miles farther, they reached the edge of Broken Mountain—what remained of it. What had once been the largest mountain in the area, one with two jagged peaks, was now a massive hill of boulders.

"Keep driving. I'll tell you when to pull off," Critch said.

Kassel weaved around large rocks, having to veer off the road to avoid rock piles. They continued through intersections and past turnoffs.

Critch opened his wrist comm to find a single message from Birk:

Pickup 05-0500 at your ping.

He let his arm rest on his thigh and leaned his head back. Critch had a ride coming for him. Day 05 was tomorrow, at five in the morning. Whoever was coming for him must already be in the sector to arrive so quickly. He needed his wrist comm on and broadcasting his signal for their sensors, but he didn't worry about CUF drones this far from Rebus Station. He found he breathed easier for the first time in weeks.

"Our ride will be here in the morning," Critch said. "So, we won't have long to wait."

"Cool." Kassel frowned. "But the docks are under CUF control. How can they pick us up without using the docks?"

"My guess? There are no safe docks for launch, so they're sending a ship equipped with drop tanks. It burns a ton of juice to make a cold launch, so you won't see many use them, especially now that all the juice plants are shut down." He kept drop tanks on the *Honorless* for a last resort scenario and had only had to use them a handful of times. He wondered if Gabe had already burned all the juice in them.

Critch squinted as he looked for the turn. "Slow down. We're getting close." Each turnoff had a sign to indicate the location. He pointed. "There it is. Take a right at A-187."

Kassel turned and immediately swerved off the road to avoid

a pile of rocks, only to drive over an even larger pile of rocks. Critch grimaced against the scraping sounds of stone against metal.

Kassel brought the truck to an abrupt stop. "Looks like this is as far as I can go."

Critch looked at the pile of rocks and brown dirt in front of them. "We're close enough. There's an entrance not too far from here."

Critch opened the door and grabbed his pack. When Kassel's door didn't open, he turned to find the boy clutching the wheel.

"Let's go," Critch said.

When Kassel turned, his expression was tight with dread. "I'm staying," he said quietly, then echoed louder, "I'm staying."

Critch raised a brow. "Oh, yeah? Want to tell me why?"

Kassel seemed to gulp down his fear. "It was what you said to May and Leony back there... about how anyone can help out, and I realized I could do more good here, finding torrents and getting them through the checkpoint, than I could up there." His eyes glanced skyward.

"You could, could you?" Critch asked.

Kassel took a deep breath. "Yeah. I could."

"It's going to be dangerous."

"I know."

Critch gave him a lengthy moment of silence before he spoke. "Well, if that's what you want—"

"It's what's right," Kassel cut in.

Critch gave him a small nod, one he hoped conveyed the pride he had in the young man and not the worry he felt about Kassel's future. He then dug into his pack and pulled out all the food and left it on the seat. "Now, don't go looking for trouble. Keep yourself safe first. You can't help anyone else if you're dead. If you do come across any torrents, there's a small tunnel right around this rock pile that didn't collapse in the explosion. It smells bad and looks even worse, but the droms don't come around here. The code is 8-4-2, the year of the Uprising. Oh, and you'll need this." He reached around his neck and pulled the chain he wore above his head. He handed it to Kassel.

Kassel stared at the pendant, wide-eyed and slack-jawed. "You're giving me a teardrop? You mean, I'm a real torrent now?"

"You became a torrent as soon as you helped save me from the droms," Critch said. "Being a torrent is about what's in your heart. I knew you'd make a fine torrent as soon as I met you."

Kassel beamed as he slid the chain around his neck. He looked at the pendant for a moment, sniffled, and then sprang across the seat and hugged Critch.

Critch held him until Kassel's embrace relaxed.

"Don't go home tonight," Critch said, "in case one of your neighbors called the droms. Do you have somewhere you can stay for a couple days?"

"Sure, I guess I can crash at Arick's."

Critch squeezed Kassel's shoulder. "Until we meet again."

Kassel sat straighter, even though his eyes were filling with tears. "Until we meet again," he repeated the fringe farewell.

Critch grabbed his pack, now much lighter without the food, and left the truck without looking back. He heard the truck lurch backward as Kassel stepped on the pedal too hard, and he smiled. That kid would make a lousy pilot, but he was one hell of a torrent.

He climbed onto the massive pile of rocks created when the bombs had shattered the mountain and started avalanches with the debris. He was careful; a twisted ankle out here could be a death sentence if his ride couldn't make it. It was a clear night, so the two moons lit up Terra as much as a Playan day.

He never understood why people—like his friend, Reyne— chose to live on the ice world. Playa was cold, dark, and grim. Even its low gravity seemed to deter colonists from moving there.

It was the opposite of warm, heavy Terra which allowed darkness only in her shadows. Yet, despite the environmental extremes, colonists from the two vastly different fringe worlds were so much alike.

Critch knew the similarities were from a hard work ethic and a need for a fair and equitable return for that work more so than where someone was born. Many citizens had forgotten what it was like to work. That was just one of the reasons he saw them as lesser humans.

As his thoughts turned darker and deadlier, Critch found himself climbing more swiftly over the rocks. He soon reached the crest. There, he scanned the collapsed mountain before him. The access point was hidden by rocks; no one would know it'd survived the blast unless they examined it up close. The rescue teams sent to dig out survivors in the hours following the bombing had found only a few accessible tunnel entrances in the rubble, and only one tunnel beyond those that had not yet collapsed. Of all the hundreds of refugees hiding in Broken Mountain the day of the attack, the rescue teams only brought home seven survivors.

After several minutes of searching, he found the entrance less than a hundred feet from where he stood. He was careful to watch his step as he made his way along the top of the rock pile toward it. When he was near, he climbed down the other side, letting gravity assist as he slid. When he reached solid ground, the entrance stood ten feet before him. The black metal door was new, having been replaced by Seda's tunnel crews following the rescue. Critch eyed the keypad on the door for only a moment before entering the three-digit code. The door opened with some scraping, and Critch wondered if the bones of the mountain weren't still settling.

The stench hit him from the darkness. He'd known the tunnels would smell from the hundreds of bodies decomposing throughout the mountain, but he'd hoped it wouldn't be so bad this far from the main tunnel network. The crews had left all the dead inside the mountain due to the instability of the collapsed tunnels and the lack of resources Terra faced after Parliament had begun to play rough with the colonies. Those victims who weren't killed instantly died trapped under and behind walls of debris.

Critch pulled up his shemagh to cover his mouth and nose, then clicked on his wrist comm's flashlight. Cranking his head around, he took one last lungful of fresh air, and then he entered the tunnel. As soon as he stepped inside, dim lights on the walls illuminated, and he realized the tunnel crews must've reestablished power to this tunnel. He clicked off his light.

Stacked near the door were boxes of water, food, and blankets, left for torrents who made it to this secret refuge. It'd be the perfect hideout, the last place the CUF would look, if not for the stench that made it a shelter of last resort.

Critch hoped he'd grow accustomed to the vile odor, but he'd been around death before and knew his olfactory response would never tame while inside. There was something about the smell of rotting flesh that turned the air to a soup that seeped into everything. The cloth covering his nose and mouth did little good. He'd be smelling death for days after he left this dank mausoleum.

A slight vibration rumbled under his feet, and he pulled out his blaster. A second later, the distant sound of rocks falling caused him to pause. He'd been right about the mountain still settling. Even though it'd been months since it was razed, he suspected small rockfalls and avalanches would continue for many more months, if not years, as sections of tunnels collapsed. The thought haunted him: he was in one of those tunnels.

Slowly, cautiously, he walked down the tunnel until it forked, with one path blocked by stone and the other, narrower path going deeper into the darkness. This part of the tunnel had been cleared, though he knew there were corpses nearby, likely just on the other side of the fallen stones.

Using his wrist comm light, he ventured down the dark tunnel long enough to see it ended with a blockage a hundred or so feet in. The narrow edge that encircled his wrist sent out light in the direction his hand pointed, causing shadows from uneven stone and pebbles to dance upon the walls as he walked.

The tunnels had first been built under Seda's grandfather's direction to mine the components needed to produce the juice that fueled all ships. Faulk Industries had been the first juice company and had thrived for three generations, though Critch suspected Seda might be its final owner.

Another vibration signaled a rockfall somewhere in the mountain, and Critch hurried back toward the entrance, where he figured was the least likely place to suffer a cave-in while he was there. He grabbed a blanket and set down his pack. He settled onto the cold, damp stone, using his pack as a pillow, and let himself fall asleep in the haunted crypt.

Critch shot awake at every vibration and sound—he seldom slept longer than an hour at a time. Growing up playing in the tunnels, he'd never had a fear of them. But, now his dreams haunted him with tight, lightless places that smothered his lungs.

An hour before his scheduled pickup time, he pushed himself to his feet. His right leg had gone numb, and his foot tingled. Every muscle was tight, and his back ached. He gave himself extra time to stretch out before grabbing his pack. He folded the blanket for the next person who needed it—he prayed someone else would make it here to use it—and opened the door.

It was still nighttime, and he deeply inhaled the fresh air that smelled of evergreens. He double-checked the door to make sure it locked behind him before he began climbing the hill of fallen rock once more.

When he reached the top, he scanned for friend or foe. Seeing neither, he took a seat and let himself enjoy watching night give way to dawn.

His ride arrived thirty minutes late. He frowned when he saw the *Scorpia* set down on the flat ground a safe distance from possible avalanches. Large drop tanks weighed it down even more on the dusty ground.

Critch slid down the rocks and ran toward the ship with both relief and trepidation: relief at being saved; trepidation at why it was the *Scorpia* that had come for him and not a different specter.

A ramp extended, and a cargo door opened. Birk emerged.

Critch hit the ramp at a jog. "You're late. Lose track of time in bed with your partner?"

"Maybe," Birk said, a wide grin climbing his face as he held out his hand to help Critch on board. He scowled. "Aw, dang, Critch, you smell awful."

"It's damned good to see you." He grabbed Birk's forearm. "But aren't you supposed to be wreaking hell on the CUF at Devil Town right now?"

Birk sobered and shook his head. "The CUF had already taken Spate."

CHAPTER 6

HAUNTED DREAMS

Broken Mountain, Terra

"SO, Heid and his lackeys are probably getting plenty cocky right about now," Critch said with a sense of dread as he climbed the *Scorpia*'s ramp. If the CUF had control of all the fringe stations, it'd believe the rebellion was finished. He added, as much to build his confidence as Birk's, "Perfect time for us to put them in their place."

"Perfect time for one of your Coastal Run-style plans," Birk said before stepping in behind Critch and climbing the ramp.

"I'm working on one," Critch said.

Birk closed the door and tapped the intercom on the wall. "Throttle, I've got Critch and we're inside."

"Good. Now, get your butts to the bridge and strap in."

"It's good to see Throttle hasn't gone all soft on you," Critch said.

Birk chuckled. "I don't think I ever have to worry about that."

Critch headed down the kinked, narrow hallway to the bridge. He knew the *Scorpia* well. He'd bought and customized the ship as part of his fleet. Once a civilian security ship, she was midsized and lacked the cargo space his larger ships had, but she more than compensated for that lack through speed and other features, making her the perfect scouting ship. Like all of Critch's specters, the *Scorpia* had been upgraded with stealth capabilities and drop tanks.

The lightning bolt-shaped hallway was difficult to maneuver at a walking pace, and Critch had to move slowly to make the sharp turns. He'd just turned sideways to move around a support beam that took up half the hallway when another man nearly plowed into him.

Critch took a step back as the man squeezed through. Critch, still wearing his pack, found himself pressed against the wall. "Whoa there, buddy. Buy me a drink first," Critch muttered as the man pushed through him and then Birk.

"Dang it, Eddy," Birk said. "Why'd you leave the engine compartment?"

"I had to pee," Eddy said and kept walking in the opposite direction of the pair without looking back.

"Your new engineer has an interesting personality," Critch said before continuing on his way.

"He was Throttle's pick," Birk said, then added, "he knows his engine stuff. Now, if only we could leave him back there all the time, then he'd make a perfect crew member."

"And the one you picked? How's he working out?"

"Garrett? He's doing great. He's young, but he's a quick learner, and he's a lot easier to talk to than Eddy."

Critch chuckled at Birk's comment about Garrett's age. Critch, only in his low forties, was still old enough to be Birk's and Throttle's father. Eddy didn't look a month over twenty. Critch trusted Birk, who'd been his right hand on the *Honorless*, which is the only reason he'd let Birk and Throttle pick their crew when he gave the *Scorpia* to Birk. He hadn't expected to find himself on a ship of kids. Not a single one of them was old enough to remember the Uprising, but maybe that was a good thing.

Fewer deaths to haunt their dreams.

When he reached the bridge, its door stood open. He stepped through, and he saw Throttle's hands flying over the screen in the pilot's chair—which was also the captain's chair on this ship... the captain's wheelchair, to be accurate. Critch had promised to pay for her back surgery, but the CUF had moved in before he'd had the chance. At least Seda had been able to get her a signal blocker to wear, which emitted "white noise" to neutralize the signal from the Myrad's transmitter. It kept her current spinal implant from going on and off, though he'd heard from Birk that the blocker was glitchy, and that transmissions from a remote control sometimes made it through.

She tossed a quick look over her shoulder. "Glad to see you could join us. Now, buckle in so we can get ourselves somewhere a little more Critch-friendly."

He took the only free seat, leaving the co-pilot seat open for Birk.

"A place like that exists?" Birk jabbed as he buckled into his seat.

Critch scowled. "Like either of you are better off."

"I'm not the one at the top of the Most Wanted list," Throttle said.

"The last I heard, your name's on the list now, too," Critch said.

Throttle wrinkled her nose. "What the hell is that smell?"

"Critch," Birk said.

"You're taking a full detox when we're clear of this sector, and those clothes are getting drifted."

"You won't hear an argument from me," Critch said.

Throttle held up her hand, silencing the bridge, and tapped the intercom. "Launch is a 'go' from the bridge. Eddy, confirm."

"*Mechanicals are green for launch*," came the engineer's reply.

"Okay everyone. Launch in thirty. Terra's heavier gravity will make this a bumpy ride. If you're not strapped in, you fix your own broken bones. Once we initiate launch, you can guaran-damn-tee the CUF will pick up our heat signature when we break gravity. Let's hope we can at least clear Terra's airspace before the CUF sends ships to tickle our fenders. Launch in twenty."

Critch entered his access code for the systems, and diagnostics lit up the screen. Not disabling his codes was one of a few stipulations he'd had when he'd offered the *Scorpia* to Birk.

"I'll have the photon guns armed and ready as soon as we break through the airspace," Birk said.

"I know you will," Throttle said without looking up.

Critch noticed she mouthed the words to whatever launch checklist she was reciting in her head. He grinned at her focus.

"Count us down, Birk," she said quickly.

"Ten..." he said.

The engines growled to life, and Critch could feel the vibrations as both thrusters began to heat the ground below them.

"Eight..."

System beeps echoed across the small bridge as they initiated their launch processes.

"Six..."

The engine noise grew louder. Critch watched the various sequences underway via the screen before him.

"Four... Looks like we're being hailed by Rebus Station docks."

"Screw them," Throttle said.

"Two..."

"Switching to drop tanks," Throttle announced.

There was a slight lull in the din from the engines.

"Launch."

The engines roared. G-forces pushed Critch down toward the floor, and he grabbed the armrests for stability. His head lowered, and he pressed it back against his headrest to fight the gravity.

The *Scorpia* lifted slowly, picking up speed and increasing G-force as it climbed. Minutes passed.

"Uh oh," Birk said. "The CUF has just notified us that we're an unauthorized launch."

"Hold on to the drop tanks, Throttle," Critch ordered.

"Why?" she asked.

Not taking the time to respond, he swiped through system screens until he reached the weapons systems. "Birk, you take the bow gun, and I'll take the stern."

"But, there's nothing out there yet," Birk said.

A proximity alarm sounded the instant the G-force gave way to weightlessness.

"Dang it," Birk muttered. "We have two bogeys—look like patrol ships—coming up at our two-four-zero on an intercept course. They'll be within no-evade range in less than three minutes."

Critch could see the incoming ships on his screen as well. Birk had prepped the gun systems. They were up, and all checks had cleared. All Critch had to do was open the bay, and his photon gun was ready to fire.

"You have enough juice for stealth?" Critch asked.

"Of course, but it won't do much good if they already have a visual."

"When you drop the tanks, put them between us and them. Then, make sure we can line up for a shot," Critch said.

"*Oh.* Now I get what you're thinking."

He felt the *thunk* of large metal arms releasing the drop tanks. The tanks drifted behind the *Scorpia* as it picked up speed. Critch tapped each tank as a bogey on his screen.

"When we blow the tanks, their tracking systems will be disrupted for only a second or two. Turn on stealth and start to fly a random pattern, and do all that within a second," Critch said.

"Already on it," Throttle said. "Just waiting for you to blow them."

Critch focused on his screen. "Taking the shots... *now*." He fired off two photon beams toward the drop tanks. Each shot was an easy hit. They connected with the drop tanks. For a split second there was nothing, then each burst outward as the juice and oxygen burned. Within an atmosphere, the explosions would be fantastic. In space, fire moved more like water, quickly morphing into a fine mist before even more quickly suffocating.

He watched his screen—as it was the only way in zero-g to see if Throttle had changed her flight path. Sure enough, she was good on her word. The *Scorpia* had veered sharply to the right with smaller changes every few seconds.

"We have enough juice to run in stealth until we make it to the yellow moon," Throttle said.

"Phobos," Critch corrected.

"What?" Throttle asked.

"That's the name of the moon. The other one is Deimos. Twin moons."

"Thanks for the astronomy lesson," Throttle said. "Now, can we get back to making sure we don't have droms snuggling up too close?"

"Looks like they're splitting up to try to get a visual on us," Birk said.

"We're far enough away, we should be safe from visual," Critch said, knowing that starlight wouldn't glint off the flat black rilon covering the ship.

"Well, if they keep coming, they'll soon find out that this *Scorpia* stings," Birk said with pizzazz.

Critch raised a brow. "How long have you been saving up that little pun?"

"He hasn't been saving it. He uses it on just about every flight," Throttle answered drily.

Critch turned back to the scanners. "They'll be sending more ships. The faster you can jump, the safer we'll be."

"We have to meet up with the others first," Throttle said.

"What others?"

"The *Night Velvet*, the *Delilah*, and the *Ocelot* are all waiting at the yellow—Phobos—for us. We'll jump together."

"What's your jump plan?" Critch asked.

Throttle shrugged. "We'll head to Darios and help out with Operation Silent Night. Everything's riding on that mission now."

"Not everything," Critch said. "I have an idea that will either pull the odds in our favor or bring hellfire down upon us. We'll work out the plans on the way. Plus, we'll need Seda's help on this job. Take us one jump to sector 863-A-2."

She frowned. "But that sector takes us away from the fringe and toward—" Her eyes widened. "You think we can take on the CUF on its own turf?"

"They don't expect us to attack them. We need to mix things up a bit."

"That's your plan?" Birk whistled. "That makes the Coastal Run look like a Sunday drive."

"I'm still working out the details," Critch said. "We won't need four specters for this mission. You can send Lou and Jake to Darios. The *Ocelot*'s crew has done a job like this before; let Miko know that he'll follow us on the jump." He paused. "I don't suppose you've heard any word from the *Honorless*?"

Birk shook his head with a somber expression. "Think the CUF took it out?"

"Not a chance. Something like that would've made the news." He took a breath to keep the anger at bay. "Gabe took it."

"Dang. That's low," Birk drawled out.

"Don't worry. I'll get her back," Critch said. A blip on his scanner showed a patrol ship had reached the edge of their area before disappearing again. "Now, get us up to the *Ocelot* and jump before the droms catch up to us."

"I'm on it," Throttle said.

"Good thing we've got all the stuff meant for Devil Town. Something tells me we'll need it," Birk said, and then he grinned. "Using it on a citizen world would be so much more fun."

Critch unbuckled and walked over to Birk's station. "Show me what you've got."

Birk pulled up an inventory file and scrolled through the list.

A smile crept up Critch's face. "It's a start."

CHAPTER 7

CHAOS MANAGEMENT

New Sol, Darios

REYNE STOOD in the command room of the small slingshot launchpad in Thunder Canyon. The launchpad was on the opposite side of Darios from Sol Base, making landings and launches possible without the CUF being the wiser... at least for the time being. The warship sitting above Sol Base was currently focusing all its resources on that colony except for patrol passes covering a five-hundred-mile radius from the colony twice per day.

With the passes taking place like clockwork, it was easy to schedule landings and takeoffs. However, all the CUF had to do was change up its timing and everything Reyne was coordinating would be at risk.

Several ships could come in at once, since they were landing on the canyon floor rather than within a space dock. Each ship would be unloaded of its cargo of soldiers and munitions, tugged to the launchpad, loaded with food, and launched.

Yesterday, when the 3D printer arrived on the *Lady Lilith*, all other transports were put on hold for the larger ship, to minimize any risk to the printer... to *Hatha's* printer. The *Lilith* currently sat under camouflage nets made of philoseed leaves. Next to her sat Reyne's ship, the *Gryphon*, where Reyne would likely find his ship's mechanic, Boden, on board, even though it needed no work. Boden was in one of his quiet moods after giving up his Sweet Soy addiction for the fourth time. Reyne suspected it wouldn't be the last time.

Sixx was outside, currently in charge of hand-to-hand combat training. Many torrents were simply colonists who'd lost their homes and livelihoods. They ranged in age from twenty to seventy. There were few younger, since the Collective required a two-year service agreement for all colonists upon reaching the age of eighteen. The few younger torrents were colonists deemed unsuitable for service, either due to a physical or mental disability. Where the Collective saw weakness, Reyne saw opportunity. His daughter, Throttle, had been excluded from service because she was a paraplegic. Yet, she had become one of the finest pilots he'd ever seen. There was James, the autistic nineteen-year-old sitting in a makeshift cubicle in the corner of Reyne's command center, who tracked the inventories so precisely that there'd yet to be a discrepancy.

The comm screen before Reyne chimed. He accepted the call and took a seat.

Seda's face appeared on the screen.

"You had me worried," Reyne said. "You were supposed to call over three hours ago."

A couple seconds lagged before Seda spoke. Interplanetary comms suffered lags, especially as the number of sectors between the two people increased.

"I just got off a comm with Critch," the Terran businessman said. "Throttle picked him up yesterday, and they're safe."

"Good," Reyne said. "Are they headed here now?"

"No. We think we have a plan to buy you the time you need to finish preparing for Silent Night."

Reyne's brows rose in surprise. "Is this one of Critch's plans?"

Seda nodded. "It is."

"Don't tell me he's dragged Throttle into his scheming."

"He has."

Reyne scowled. "I already don't like the sound of it."

The CUF was celebrating a preeminent victory over the torrents after taking Rebus Station and Devil Town. With Ice Port bombed to hell and the CUF already in control of Sol Base, the torrent leaders worried the CUF would change its game from invading colonies to hunting down the remaining torrents. In response, Vym had led the sleight of hand of displaying an abundance of traffic in and out of the Space Coast. The ploy was working. The CUF disliked flying into the asteroid belt, since the rocks battered their larger ships. Instead, they'd stationed patrols to monitor movement, believing they were keeping tabs on the rebellion.

As sure as vigs stank, they'd figure out that the torrents weren't running. Reyne doubted he had a month to prep for the mission to reclaim Sol Base, dubbed Operation Silent Night. He'd been crunching numbers and talking with Seda and Vym every day to discuss the schedules and possible backup plans. To hear they had something that could take some of the pressure off relieved him. Many deaths could be prevented.

Reyne sighed. "All right. Tell me about it."

"They're heading to Myr..."

By the time Seda finished sharing everything he knew, Reyne's blood boiled with anger. Critch was on a suicide run, and he was taking Throttle with him.

"That is the worst plan I've ever heard," Reyne said.

"That's what you say about every plan," Seda said before he shrugged. "We can turn the war back to our favor by taking Sol

Base, but if Critch's plan works, we give the Collective something to fear."

"I wish I had your level of confidence, but I've seen too many operations go sideways when the action starts," Reyne said.

"I'm counting on your trust more so than your optimism, Aramis. Silent Night is the most important mission in the war. If we can't reclaim Sol Base, then Parliament will win, and all our heads will be on pikes."

"It's not my head I'm worried about," Reyne said. "It's Throttle's head and the head of every other colonist's kid out there."

"Have faith," Seda said. "When I blew my plants, the Collective's financial foundation cracked. When we cut off their food supplies from Darios, the Collective will crumble practically overnight. They won't be forced to negotiate; they'll be forced to surrender."

Seda looked offscreen for a moment before turning back to Reyne. "Looks like I need to get on another comm. I'll talk to you tomorrow."

"Same scheduled time?"

"Let's plan on it," Seda said, which meant he'd likely be at least an hour late.

Reyne couldn't blame Seda for his tardiness. The man was hiding on an asteroid that was serving as the central communications and coordination hub for the entire torrent movement.

A chime sounded and Reyne looked down. He cut the connection with Seda and tapped his wrist comm. Sixx's visage came into view.

"What's up?" Reyne asked.

"We've got another tussle out here at Warehouse Three. Seems that a Spaten expected a bit more variety than cavote cakes now that he's on Darios, and a Darion seemed to think he's being rather ungrateful, being a 'guest' and all."

"I'll be right there," Reyne said and headed for the door. On the way out, he typed a quick message to Tully, Hatha's head of security, who was currently in the area. The infighting and arguments were increasing every day. The torrents were arriving hungry and ready for action. The Darions had spent months volunteering their time and energy to build the launchpad, and just when they thought they'd get a break, they were asked to work double shifts—which meant even more time away from their fields.

Both groups of colonists were scraping by. Both craved independence, and both were going to drive Reyne crazy.

CHAPTER 8

SHATTERED ICE

Above Ice Port, Playa

BARRETT ANDERS DREADED ANSWERING the comm. Every conversation with his commanding officer left him even more frustrated about his current situation. He hadn't complained when he'd been ordered to his destroyer—the *Caliban*—to stand watch over the ghost town of Ice Port. After the fateful day at Parliament, he'd known he'd be shoved off to some sector where he could cause little damage to Senator Heid's war-making plans.

Playa, the planet farthest from the Collective's pair of citizen worlds, was a natural choice. Barrett's predecessor, Corps General Michel Ausyar, had bombed the planet's fringe station and space docks into oblivion in an attempt to quell the fringe riots, though Barrett suspected there'd been more to it than that.

After the bombing, the only life believed to remain on the planet was the scattered colonies of stretches, unnaturally tall humans who'd lived in low-g for too long to be able to survive anywhere else.

However, Barrett had seen enough to know there was far more life on Playa than Parliament believed. The *Caliban*'s scanners had picked up ships landing and launching a few hundred miles from where Ice Port had stood. Only a handful of ships in the Collective had the ability to launch without the assistance of space docks, which meant there was likely an unknown space dock on Playa's surface.

He suspected that he'd discovered the torrent base, but he wanted to be careful with that knowledge until he better understood the approach that would be best for the entire system. He'd announced to the tech who'd caught the first signals that they were relief aid workers and to mark the area off as a relief zone, exempting it from further scans. That order could earn him another demotion if the wrong person found out. He trusted the tech because she was a conscript, but he knew both Laciam and Heid had spies on board the *Caliban*, reporting all of Barrett's actions to their leaders.

He missed the *Littorio*. He'd led that crew for years and knew who could be trusted. Unfortunately, that warship was now commanded by someone under Heid's thumb, while Barrett had an aged destroyer with an inexperienced crew of unknown loyalties. The only positive in his current situation was that he didn't have to sit under the *Unity*'s shadow. At least, out here in the black, he felt at relative peace.

His comm screen chimed again, and he took a deep breath before tapping the *Accept* button.

Laciam's smug, Myrad features filled the screen. "Commandant Anders, I was beginning to think you wouldn't answer."

"My apologies, Corps General. I had a problem in Engineering to address. The *Caliban*'s over fifty years old, and I have systems erroring out every day."

"All ships in the Collective Unified Forces are maintained per regulations," Laciam recited.

"I'm sure we're just experiencing glitches," Barrett said. "At least it keeps the crew busy. They get antsy with nothing to do."

"It's your lucky day, Commandant. I have a mission for you."

Barrett tensed. "The *Caliban* is at your disposal."

"Of course it is," Laciam said before continuing. "I have received intel that Vym Patel, a known torrent leader, survived the bombing of Ice Port and is still on Playa."

"Do you have a location?"

"I am sending the coordinates to you now."

Barrett pulled up the map over Laciam's face to find what he'd expected: a circle around the secret space dock in the canyon range. "Would you like me to send patrols to verify?"

"No need. I have confidence in the intel." Laciam's eyes narrowed. "Have you ever seen any activity in that area?"

Laciam was a lousy liar—it was obvious his spies had already apprised him the *Caliban* had picked up signals in that area. However, if Laciam admitted such, he'd be admitting he spied on his own officers. Barrett spoke smoothly. "Yes. I picked up minor civilian activity. I had follow-up scans conducted, but everything checked out as relief ships. I gave it little more thought since CAHP ships are the only ones sanctioned to enter Playa's airspace."

"Commandant," Laciam said with a thick tone of condescension. "Those weren't CAHP ships. Those were torrent ships, and you should've blasted them out of the sky."

"My apologies."

Laciam waved him off. "There's a reason you were demoted. You don't have good judgment. A good officer would've seen through their ruse."

"What is the mission?" Barrett asked, trying to keep the comm—and Laciam's reprimands—as brief as possible.

"You are to bomb the coordinates and then personally verify that no torrents are left alive on the surface."

"In that zone," Barrett added.

"What?"

"I wanted to clarify that I am to verify that there are no survivors on the surface in the bomb zone; not that there are no survivors on the surface of Playa."

Laciam scowled. "Of course, that's what I meant. The stretches aren't a threat to us, so there's no need to use valuable resources in eradicating them."

"Understood. I can initiate the mission today and apprise you of the results within thirty hours."

Laciam gave a nod. "You do that, and I expect logs of the full operation at the time of your report-in."

"Of course. I'll talk with you tomorrow," Barrett said.

Laciam cut the feed, and the screen went blank.

Barrett leaned back in his chair and rubbed his temples. Laciam had no leadership skills. His lineage and connections with the right people were the only reasons the Myrad was an officer rather than a tech tucked away in a back room. Gabriela Heid should've killed Laciam when he was her first officer rather than set him and the others loyal to him adrift in a patrol ship. Her act of kindness was now causing Barrett many headaches.

He pushed to his feet and headed to the bridge. There, he stood for a long moment, watching the ice world in the view panel spanning the bridge's entire front wall. Playa was the smallest of the Collective worlds. It was also the coldest, with temperatures never reaching as high as zero degrees Celsius. With its red patches of algae-like tholins, Playa looked almost welcoming, but Barrett had no desire to stand on its frigid surface. However, that was exactly what he'd be doing shortly.

He sighed and took his captain's chair. He then tapped the intercom button on the screen in front of him to speak to everyone on board. "Crew of the *Caliban*, this is your captain speaking. We have received a mission from Corps General

Laciam that we will carry out today. All second shift crew will be active during the mission, with third shift on standby. We have received the coordinates of a possible torrent target, which we are to bomb posthaste. The coordinates have been fed to all squad leaders' and officers' wrist comms. From now until after the mission, I'm declaring a communications blackout so there's no risk of torrents on the ground picking up any incoming or outgoing comms. In the meantime, be patient and be prepared. The Collective is counting on us."

"Is a blackout wise, sir?" Johns, a communications tech, asked. "If CUF Command can't reach us, they may worry the torrents destroyed our ship."

Barrett eyed the tech. *So, you're the spy.* "I have reason to believe the torrents are monitoring our comms. Even though our comms are encrypted, if the torrents see increased chatter coming from a ship that's been sitting quiet, they may get suspicious."

"Of course, sir," Johns replied quickly.

Barrett strode over to the tech who'd picked up the original signals from the canyon. "Tully, per standard procedure, I need you to log the mission."

"Of course, sir," she replied.

"Afterward, we'll review it together before sending. Understood?"

She frowned but then nodded. "Yes, sir."

Barrett patted her shoulder and then met with each of his officers to finalize plans. When he'd finished, he stood at the center of the bridge as the first phase cannon blast blazed a path toward Playa.

"Should I fire again, captain?" the gunner asked.

"No," Barrett replied. "Give it some time."

"Sir, I'm picking up a launch," Tully announced.

"Should I fire upon it?" the gunner asked.

Barrett set a timer. "No. They're evacuating. That ship is

likely full of refugees. Do you want us on the news for killing a ship full of women and children?"

"No, sir."

Barrett wasn't disobeying orders; he was simply following them precisely as Laciam had laid them out. Bomb the coordinates, Finish off any survivors *on the surface.* Laciam had mentioned nothing about engaging ships. He knew Laciam would hear about it, but Barrett's career had stalled the moment Heid demoted him. Laciam could court-martial him, but that would enrage the silent majority already in favor of peace. Barrett could always pull a Gabriela Heid and run off with his ship. But that wasn't his style.

The bridge crew threw anxious glances his way while they waited in silence for their next order. Four minutes later, another ship launched. *A single slingshot launchpad, then.*

"Sir?" the gunner asked.

"Let it pass. Our mission is to disable infrastructure, not target civilians," Barrett said. He set the timer again. Four minutes later, another ship launched, and he let it pass.

The citizens looked at him with slack-jawed expressions of shock while the conscripts eyed him as though they were trying to figure him out.

"You fired a warning shot so they could escape," Johns said. Barrett eyed the technician, and Johns added on, "Sir."

"A word, Johns," Barrett said.

Without waiting for a response, he led the way to the planning room just off the bridge. As soon as the pair stepped inside and the door closed, Barrett turned on the technician.

"You have a problem following my orders, Johns?" Barrett asked.

"No, sir. I'm only concerned that we're letting torrents escape," he said in a rush.

"We could be, but it's worth the risk."

"What risk? You think bad publicity could hurt public opinion of the war? We've already won. We're just tying up loose ends."

Barrett chuckled. "You really think that? Until the war is over, there are no winners. And public opinion matters, in time of peace and especially in time of war. But that's not the risk I was referring to. I'm talking about mutiny."

Johns frowned.

Barrett gave him a hard look. "Seventy-eight percent of this crew are colonists. We were walking a fine line before, having them police those who could be their own relatives. When we extended their terms of service, we crossed that line. The conscripts are seconds away from taking over the *Caliban*, and there's little we could do to stop it, not if they have it planned out. If we bombed fringe ships with innocents on board, I can guarantee you and I and every other citizen on this ship will be drifting out there with the debris not long after. Do you understand now?"

Johns swallowed. "Yes, sir."

Johns was cocky, like so many other citizens. He'd never been required to do anything. He'd chosen to join the CUF. He could never understand what being conscripted meant to a colonist. The ratio of colonists to citizens on every ship was similar. Every commandant, and the Corps General especially, should be shaking in their boots. They likely never even considered that the greatest risk to the CUF was already aboard their ships.

Barrett walked to the door, pausing before opening it. "Oh, and Johns?"

"Yes, sir?"

"If you send one more comm to Laciam without me seeing it first, I'll drift you myself."

Johns blanched.

Barrett turned and headed back to the bridge. He checked his timer. Six minutes had passed. "Have any other ships launched?"

"No, sir," Tully announced.

He turned to the gunner. "Fire at will."

"That's the last ship," Jed Baptiste said as he pushed back from the launchpad controls.

"I don't know who's commanding that destroyer, but fate smiled on us today," Vym said as she gripped his shoulder. "I'm still finding it hard to believe we were able to launch everyone. May their journey to Nova Colony be as fortuitous as their departure from here."

Jed stood and wrapped his arms around her waist. "I wish you would've gone with them."

She *harrumphed*. "And leave you to run the launchpad on your own? You know me, I could never stand to not micromanage."

His smile grew. "I couldn't help but notice that you did look over my shoulder the entire time."

He bent down and kissed her. She pulled him tight against her, and they stood there in a love-felt embrace.

"I knew Mason would eventually find me," she said, referring to Gabriel Heid by his Founder code name.

"But not before we finished the *Matador*."

She smiled. "Yes, that's the future."

She pressed her head against his shoulder, and they began to dance to an unwritten love song that played perfectly in their minds.

A bright flash of light filled the room, then nothing.

CHAPTER 9

BAD NEWS TRAVELS AT LIGHTNING SPEED

New Sol, Darios

"WE LOST TULAN BASE," Seda said, his somber mood clear even through the comm screen.

Reyne felt the blood drain from his face. "All those people..."

"We got lucky. Nearly everyone was evacuated. They're on their way to Nova Colony as we speak." Seda gave Reyne a pained look. "Vym and Jed stayed at the launch controls to make sure everyone got out in time. I'm sorry. I know you were close."

"It's not the first time she died," Reyne said flippantly, before sobering. "At least she was with Jed when the time came."

There was a lengthy pause before Seda spoke. "Fortunately we were in the process of moving everything from there to Darios. Our material losses could've been a lot worse. As it is, we lost a printer and two warehouses full of munitions, not to mention three tons of food. But if we'd been one week later in moving the stocked *Matador* and two printers..."

"It's still a major loss," Reyne countered. "We're down to just one launchpad that the droms don't know about, and New Sol won't stay a secret for long. There's been so much activity, it's just a matter of time before the CUF's onto us."

"You just have to hold out until we can retake Sol Base."

Reyne blew out a breath. "Well, we've been wondering about when they'd switch gears from focusing on the fringe stations to hunting us down. Are you safe?"

"No one's safe, but I'm in the safest place I can be. Only a handful of people know this asteroid exists, and even fewer people know its location. You and Critch are at a greater risk of being found."

"I'm not that important. You're the one holding the fringe together."

Seda belted out a loud laugh. "I'm just playing the role of politician right now. I put on a strong face and tell a good story, but everyone knows the two torrent marshals are what's keeping us fighting."

Reyne smiled. "You *are* a politician with the stories you weave." His features straightened. "I'm loading the *Henry Fitzroy* with food and several techs to help you out with the code we need for Silent Night."

"Good. Give Will my coordinates just before he launches. The less anyone who's on the ground here knows, the safer we all are." He paused briefly. "I want you to know, I'm also pulling in a hacker to help."

Reyne frowned. "Not the same one who designed Mason's program that killed Gabriela?"

Seda pursed his lips before speaking. "Vapor? Yeah, the one and the same. She's the best hacker in the Collective and can be trusted as long as you're the highest bidder."

"And if you're not?"

"Then you can trust her to screw you over." Seda swallowed. "She's a risk, but she's a known risk. We need the code, and if anyone can work it out in time, it's Vapor."

Reyne gave him a doubtful look.

The corners of Seda's lips curled. "Trust me, I don't plan to let her off the hook for killing Gabriela. The way I see it, Vapor's just as responsible as Mason is for her death."

Reyne nodded in agreement before changing the subject. "Any word on Critch and Throttle?"

"Everything's on track. They should make it to Myr tomorrow."

His back ached with tension. Two high-risk missions in play at the same time meant stress clung to him and seeped heavily into his gut. "I have eight specters here for the operation, but if Critch needs the firepower..."

"They won't be able to help him. You, however, need all the firepower you can get. I can see what else I can scrounge up if you need."

"I sure wouldn't turn anything down." Reyne stretched his legs to relieve the tension, but it did no good. "If you can find something, make it sooner versus later. With the CUF switching gears, we've got to be ready. Wish me luck; I'm off to talk with Hatha about bumping up our timeline."

CHAPTER 10

STRANGE BEDFELLOWS

Space, outside Myr's EMP net

"LINKING IN THREE... TWO... ONE..." Throttle's words were followed by a loud sound of metal latching onto metal.

Critch unbuckled and was out of his seat before the safety lights turned green. Nearby, less than a mile away, the *Ocelot* was still going through the same linking procedures with a ship identical to the one the *Scorpia* had just attached to.

Throttle smiled as she ran her hands over her screens, likely running more safety checks. "I've never flown a Dirac before. I heard they're so advanced, they practically fly themselves. Think they'll let me take the controls?"

"Not a chance. You're a colonist; they're citizens," Critch said. When she scowled, he added, "You could just take it."

She watched him for a second before her lips curled upward. She was considering it. He wondered if he should be proud or worried about guiding Reyne's daughter toward a life of piracy.

She turned back to her screen and tapped the intercom.

"Eddy, all checks are clear. The *Scorpia*'s yours until I get back. Take good care of her."

"*You got it, boss,*" came a response via the intercom.

Critch glanced at Birk, who was checking his weapons. The younger man didn't seem one bit bothered that the crew was looking to Throttle as the captain rather than to Birk. Not that Critch was surprised. Birk had been the best right hand he'd had, but the man had never showed much interest in leading a crew. Throttle obviously did.

Throttle pushed back in her wheelchair and stood, holding the armrest until she became steady on her feet. Critch did a double take, then realized she was wearing powered leg braces.

He motioned toward the devices that allowed her to move without a chair. "How're they working for you?"

She looked down at her legs. "Good, except they're not very comfortable. I think the hardest part is still getting my legs used to the concept of walking."

"I'll get you a spinal implant," he said. "I gave you my word."

"First, I have to take care of the one already in my back," she said before turning and heading off the small bridge.

He and Birk followed her through the hallway and to the cargo door at the back of the ship. The light above the wall panel was green, and Throttle visually double-checked the connection through the window before opening the door. A second passed, and the door to the other ship opened to reveal three smiling citizens. All three were Myrads, the bluish hue of their argyric skin making their heritage obvious. They wore colorful clothes, and the blasters in holsters on their thighs looked incongruous with their demeanors and glamour.

"Hello," the young man in front of the group said. "I'm Yang Liu, owner and captain of the *Liu-Liu-1*, and these are my friends, Ted and Ali. We're here to help you start a revolution."

He motioned to his left and then his right as he introduced his compatriots.

Critch kept himself from rolling his eyes. These three youngsters were clearly radicals, anxious to change the worlds with their idealistic views. If he hadn't needed these citizens and their ships, Critch would've sent them packing. Radicals were dangerous for two reasons: first, they were obstinate about taking orders, and second, they'd rush in when they should take things slow. He suspected he'd have trouble with this group on both counts.

"I'm Drake Fender," Critch said, using his real name, since most citizens would be unfamiliar with his nickname.

"You're even scarier-looking in person. I've never seen someone with so many scars before," Ali said with a touch of awe in her voice.

Critch ignored her. "And this is Throttle and Birk."

"Throttle?" Yang asked. "That's an odd name. Is that your real name?"

"No," Throttle replied.

"We have several crates to move onto your ship," Critch said. "Help us move them so we can get this operation started."

The trio seemed surprised at first. He suspected none of them had ever been asked to lift cargo in their lives.

"Oh, of course," Yang said, and then waved his friends forward.

After several minutes of entertaining—and frustrating—hauling of cargo onto the Dirac, the six people stood inside the *Liu-Liu-1*, with Eddy giving them a thumbs-up through the window of the *Scorpia*.

"I hope you can trust him better than I could trust Gabe," Critch said when Throttle waved farewell to her crew member.

"Eddy would never steal the *Scorpia*. If he had to captain it, he'd have to deal with people every time he had to resupply." She grinned. "But I know he's going to love having the ship alone to himself for a few days."

"He won't be alone," Birk said. "The *Ocelot*'s mechanic is staying behind, too. I bet they'll spend hours talking about Flux engines and the right thickness of rilon for the most efficient jump."

Throttle chuckled. "You're right. The only thing he likes better than being alone is talking with someone who speaks his language."

"If you'd please follow me," Yang began. "We'll be more comfortable on the bridge."

They turned from the *Scorpia* and followed their host through the spacious ship. The Dirac was a luxury yacht and reminded Critch of the *Honorless* before he started modifying it.

Yang motioned down a hallway. "Unfortunately, this is only a five-bedroom ship and, as you can see, there are six of us..."

"No problem," Throttle said. "Birk and I share a room."

Yang's face lifted. "Oh, excellent. Then, please select from the two remaining rooms. I hope they are sufficient for your needs."

Throttle chuckled, probably because on the *Gryphon* and the *Scorpia*, she would've had little more than a bunk. Critch suspected Birk and she were going to take full advantage of having an actual bedroom for once.

"The bridge is this way," Yang said as he continued the tour. "The dining area is off to your right here. We eat together, and you'll find Ted makes the best tuna pasta in the entire system."

"I wouldn't go that far," Ted said, blushing. "But I am rather proud of it."

"We're not moving in," Critch said. "You're just giving us a lift to and from Myr."

The citizens sobered, and Yang turned to face Critch. "We're going with you. When you blow up Parliament, we're going with you."

Critch's jaw slackened. "Seda told you the mission?"

Yang's chin lifted. "He told Mother because he trusts her."

Critch rubbed his face. "How many others know? Cousins? Your friends' cousins?"

"Just Mother and the five of us who volunteered for this important mission."

Critch sighed. "Too many people know. This mission's scrubbed."

"No!" Yang reached out and grabbed Critch's forearm, only to release it like Critch's skin was on fire when he saw Critch's glare. "You can trust us. Seda trusts us. Doesn't that say a lot?"

"Is your mother a Founder?" Critch asked.

"A what?" Yang asked.

"Never mind."

"Mother was Gaia Welden's best friend."

"Who's Gaia Welden?" Critch asked.

Yang blinked. "Seda's wife. I mean, they kept it a secret from everyone, but Mother knew, of course, because—like I said—they were best friends. When Seda told Mother that Senator Heid killed Gaia to get to him, we all wanted vengeance. Gaia was loved by everyone she met on Myr. The word's already getting out that Gabriel Heid had something to do with her death, and that's garnering him quite a few enemies. So, now do you understand that you can trust us?"

"We'll see first how the next several hours go."

"They'll go fine," Yang said, brushing him off. "And then we'll waltz you right up the front steps of the Parliament building."

Critch chuckled. "With this face?"

"Well, you'll have to look like Myrads first," Yang said. "Ali's an actress and does great with stage makeup. She's going to turn all three of you into Myrads."

Critch turned his gaze to the woman.

Ali swallowed as she looked from Critch's scarred face to Throttle's braces. "We have our work cut out for us." Then she tacked on quickly, "But I can do it. You'll look like any other Myrad when I'm done with you."

"There you have it," Yang said with a smile. "Mother is a senator, and she'll have us cleared as visitors by the time we arrive."

Critch still didn't like the idea of working with four citizens on such an important mission, but he found his confidence growing at hearing their plan. "Okay," he said after a lengthy pause. "But you will not touch those blasters without my express permission. Got it?"

"Of course," Yang said, excitement rushing his words. His two friends nodded energetically.

"Good. Now, let's get to the bridge. Miko's cargo and crew should be loaded by now."

The two trios made it to the bridge.

"Wow," Throttle said on a sigh.

"*Liu-Liu* has all the latest upgrades," Yang said with clear pride. "For my birthday this year, I added a Chirp 2300."

"I didn't think those transponders were even out yet," Throttle said as she grabbed the chair nearest Yang.

He gave her a sly smile. "They aren't. I know a guy who knows a guy."

Yang took the captain's chair, made obvious by being larger and plusher than the other chairs on the bridge. He tapped the transmitter. "This is *Liu-Liu-1* calling *Liu-Liu-2*. Quit slacking off over there."

"How'd you score the *1* and he get stuck with the *2*?" Critch asked with some humor.

Yang tapped his chest. "Simple. I'm six minutes older than Wang."

Critch's brows lifted. "Wang? Yang? Your mother gave you those names?"

Yang pouted. "Those are highly respected family names. They've been passed down for over eight generations."

"I'll never get those two straight. You need a nickname," Critch muttered.

Before Yang spoke, a transmission came through. *"This is the* Liu-Liu-2. *We've been ready for thirty minutes, waiting on your lazy bums."*

Throttle chuckled and spoke softly to Birk. "Bums. He actually said, 'bums.' These blue-skins are so adorable."

Ali shot Throttle a glare, but Throttle didn't seem to notice.

"Let's jump in ninety," Yang said. "See you suckers on the other side."

"Jump in ninety confirmed. See you, sucker."

As Yang worked the controls, Critch tried to access systems but couldn't see anything beyond instructional guides. He pushed the screen away and turned his attention back to the Dirac's captain.

"How sure are you that your access codes won't raise any red flags? I'd lay bets not too many citizens are going for pleasure cruises lately."

"I'm one hundred percent sure," Yang replied. "We do this all the time."

Critch raised a brow.

"I mean, we fly out beyond the nets all the time," Yang clarified. "Wang and I are geocachers. We take jumps every couple of days searching for caches and setting up new ones. There's this one cache in Crito's Belt that we've been hunting for over three years. Anyway, a couple hours ago, we logged a quick cache on a transformer station to cover our tracks in case some tech gets snoopy. As soon as we jump, I'll reprogram my transponder to show we went straight from the cache to the net."

Critch gave a small nod. "You know, you seem to have a pretty decent head on your shoulders for a citizen, Chirp."

Yang grinned broadly, and then frowned. "Chirp?"

"It's a good nickname," Ted said with a snicker. "You do talk a lot."

"Hey, wait until I come up with a name for you," Yang, or Chirp, snapped back.

"I don't need one. My name is original."

"Oh, yeah. 'Ted' is really original."

"All right. Enough," Critch said. "Focus on making the jump and getting us through that electromagnetic pulse net. When this is all done, you can call each other whatever you want."

Yang's face hardened. "I'll get you through the EMP. You can count on me."

CHAPTER 11

DOGMATIC DECISIONS

Parliament, Myr

GABRIEL HEID WAS GROWING tired of inept underlings. Every day, he spent more hours supervising others' duties than keeping an ear to each of the colonies. He had to remind himself that he needed patience for just a bit longer. He'd devoted his entire life to strengthening the Collective. He'd sacrificed everything and everyone he loved to see his vision become a reality. The war would be over soon, as he'd projected, and the Collective would be stronger than ever once his Forces established profitable control over the colonies and, thus, the Collective overall.

Heid had desired an upheaval. Statistically, civilizations prospered when a significant conflict took place once every generation. But Seda Faulk had escalated what should've been a series of straightforward riots for equal rights into a war for independence. The rogue had caused unnecessary deaths and expenses, and it would take years for the Collective to recover from the recession the torrents' antics had brought on. As a result, Heid had to adjust his plans and forcibly take control of all the fringe stations, stretching the CUF's resources more thinly than expected.

Citizens were drastically outnumbered by colonists, especially within the CUF. He'd been fortunate the operations had gone swiftly, but as long as Seda was alive, the torrents could still complicate Heid's plans. He didn't want to kill the Terran—Seda's death would inspire additional revolts that the CUF would then have to expend further resources to quell—but the time had come that Seda's death, and its aftermath, was a necessity to ensure success.

He opened the desk drawer to his left to reveal a small safe. After entering a ten-digit passcode, the door slid open to reveal a single tablet. He pulled out the tablet that was known to himself and very few others. After going through the security protocols, he tapped out a message that needed few words.

Ranger—
  Approval granted to terminate Aeronaut.
  For the free...
  —Mason

Heid closed the tablet and returned it to his desk safe, pushed to his feet, and strode to his office door. All senators had offices on the second floor, though the offices of the co-chairs—Heid and Etzel—were the largest and most opulent, larger than most fringe homes.

Parliament looked more like a castle than a government building, courtesy of the Myrad architect who'd designed the structure. Alluvians generally took more to clean lines and open spaces. Heid prided himself on embracing both cultures in his environment. Classical silver pieces—but not too many—sat atop Alluvian bamboo tables.

He wiped a fingerprint from a one-of-a-kind casting of a fishing vessel. He'd liked the art piece so much that he'd paid the artist to destroy his cast, ensuring only Heid could savor that particular specimen.

He left his office within the Parliament building and hadn't walked more than five feet from his office before his assistant rushed forward.

"Senator, I need your signature."

Heid stopped. "Of course you do, Jasmine." He pressed his thumbprint over at least a dozen forms and letters before handing the tablet back. "I've often said that when it comes to politics, the size of the thumbprint is far more important than the volume of the voice."

"You are a wise man," she said before changing the subject. "They've finished the wall. It's stunning. Have you seen it?"

"I was heading there before you stopped me."

Jasmine shrank. "My apologies, Senator."

He squeezed her shoulder. "No need to apologize. You're doing your job, and you're doing a fine job at that."

"Thank you, Senator."

He continued on his stroll down the long hallway lined with portraits of previous senators and other leaders who'd played crucial roles in establishing and guiding the Collective. The heels of his shined shoes made sharp snaps with each strike to the floor, echoing through the empty hallway. The sounds were rhythmic, almost meditational, until he slowed, then stopped, at the top of the massive staircase that led down to the first floor, where the chamber for sessions stood.

Like the rest of the building, the chamber would be empty, with Parliament currently on a two-day break. Nearly all senators were at various social events, mingling with the public and getting votes for the next election. Heid no longer worried about such things. Delivering on his promises of a short war to bring order back to the Collective would ensure that he would remain co-chair of Parliament. However, he'd never been fond of the concept of co-chairing, and his next project was to enable the senators to understand that a single chair of Parliament would be far more beneficial to the Collective, especially if he were to be the one to prove it. Etzel was too old and no longer had the stomach to make hard decisions for the benefit of the Collective. While Etzel was easy enough to control, everything would be easier without having to deal with the bureaucratic red tape that came with sharing leadership.

Leading people was exhausting. He longed to return to his home on Alluvia, if only for a few days. He missed the sound of waves lapping against the shore. He'd built his Myrad house on the shore, but there were no waves on Myr. The stillness gave the world a sense of lifelessness, even though the planet teemed with life. He'd even gone so far as to have ambient sounds of waves play throughout his Myrad house, but they were shallow echoes of an ocean's breath.

He'd travel home as soon as he could bring closure to the conflicts bringing stress to the Collective. Until then, he would tirelessly continue his mission.

The doors leading outside had been designed like the rest of the building—overdone and ostentatious. They were transparent, with veins of silver that drew famous scenes from the Collective's history, drawing one, then morphing seconds later to draw the next. Heid had passed through these doors for over thirty years and had each scene memorized: first came the colonization of Alluvia, then Myr, then the fringe, then finally, the emergence of United Day. The doors were one of the few features he truly enjoyed about the building.

He stepped outside and down the steps, turning around

when he had a full view. He smiled. He now had another feature to appreciate. On the wall to the left of the doors was a holographic video displaying the images of five Myrads, each with their name listed beneath their image: *Edmun Strand – Michael Travers – Margine Travers – Nannette Noun – Josef Romenko.* Above the video, five stars were emblazoned in silver. Below, the text read:

In the 764th year of the Collective, five unarmed citizens were brutally murdered by radical colonists while administering to children in poverty on a humanitarian mission via the Citizens Against Hunger Program. Their deaths, known as the Rebus Station Tragedy, led to the Resilience War to bring peace across the Collective's six worlds.

Heid gave a nod to the artist's excellent work. This memorial would help shape history. Within a generation, citizens would think of that memorial when they thought of how the Resilience War began. There would be no records of citizens protesting the treatment of the colonies. Instead, the records would be slanted toward the colonies trying to overpower the citizen worlds. Videos of the fringe riots. The true value of history wasn't in its accuracy, but rather in how it could shape minds toward the right future.

Humans, by their very nature, were tribal and competitive beasts. They needed a common enemy to hate in order to work together and thrive. The Earth system had attempted to build a world based on equality, but every experiment in democracy had failed after two hundred years. Heid had studied and knew that for the Collective to succeed for millennia, the colonists would need to hate the citizens and vice versa. That was the only way.

"Senator Heid, I must speak with you," a woman called out from behind him.

He sighed, turned, and put on his politician's smile. "Ah, Senator Liu. It's always a pleasure to see you." He cocked his head. "I thought you'd be at Legacy Starporation's Grand Opening at Smithton today."

She approached, carrying a large green plant. "I was, until I heard Corps General Laciam is taking the *Unity* to the fringe worlds tomorrow."

"He is."

She moved the plant to rest on her hip, but it did little to help her look serious. "Myr and Alluvia need protection. We need to keep at least two warships here."

He held up his hand in a show of placation. "How about we go to my office to discuss this?"

"I would like that," she said. "Oh, but let's go to my office. I picked this plant up at the Smithton Market this morning and need to water it. It's a Dieffenbachia Exotica. Isn't it lovely?"

"It is," Heid mused. Then, he held out his hands. "Here, let me carry that for you, Luna."

She smiled warmly. "Thank you, Gabriel."

Their conversation became easy, and they headed inside.

CHAPTER 12

THE GUNPOWDER PLOT

Parliament, Myr

THE GROUP of Myrads approached the Parliament building, and their reflections were made clearly in the smooth glass.

Critch nearly scowled. He looked like a viggin' Myrad. He had to admit, Ali was an artist with makeup. He couldn't even see his scars, though he didn't even recognize himself through the silicon muck she'd used on his face and neck.

Birk snickered as he looked at his reflection.

"I hope no one gets a picture of us like this," Throttle muttered at his side.

"Hey, I think I did pretty good," Ali said.

"Yeah, you did *too* good," Throttle said. "I look like one of you."

Critch agreed. While all Throttle's skin had needed was a tint of blue added, her hair had been colored to a deep purple, since Myrads had an unnatural obsession with bright colors. A long, silky, colorful coat hid her leg braces, and Critch was relieved to see that Throttle had become acclimated to walking a normal stride.

"You all look good," Yang said. "Now, straighten up. Mother is ready for us."

Yang turned and walked up to the comm screen embedded in stone to the right of the doors. He held out his wrist comm, and a light ran over it. An automated, slightly robotic voice came through the speaker.

"Welcome, Citizen Yang Liu. We have you listed in a group of six visitors for Senator Luna Liu today as part of your school project. Is that correct?"

"Yes," Yang replied. "We're interviewing her for our Political Science class."

"Excellent. Each of your friends must have their wrist comm scanned, and then you may proceed into the building. Should you need assistance while inside, approach any wall screen."

Yang nodded toward Critch, who approached first and held out his comm. He focused on not holding his breath while the light shone over the comm that had a thin piece of tech clinging to the screen that would feed faulty data to any scanner. A human could notice the slight variation, which looked like a polarized screen had been taped over the comm, but computers only noticed what they were programmed to notice.

"Welcome, Citizen David Smithton. You're cleared to enter the building."

Critch breathed easier as he stepped back for the remaining four to be processed. A hologram on the other side of the doors caught his gaze, and he found himself reading the so-called memorial. He cursed under his breath. Leave it to politicians to lie about what had started the war. *Five citizens.* The memorial said nothing about the tens of thousands of colonists that had been slaughtered.

"We're all clear," Yang said.

Critch turned to see everyone waiting. "Let's go," he said.

They proceeded. The large doors opened. Yang led the way, followed by the three torrents, Ali, and Ted. Critch noticed no weapons sensors as he passed through, and he looked around, still seeing none. The fringe stations had sensors at every entrance. That Parliament didn't have any meant they assumed no attack would come from the ground. Between patrol ships and the EMP nets enwrapping each citizen world, the two planets were safe from colonist attacks. They assumed citizens would never attack their own if they were kept well fed and rich.

They were about to learn differently.

"Mother is on the second floor," Yang said as he took the first steps on the massive staircase. "She arrived twenty minutes before us."

At the top of the stairs, they turned.

"It's so quiet," Birk said.

"The entire place clears out when they're on break. Even human security gets the time off," Yang said, just before stopping at an office door. On the comm screen near the door was the face of an attractive Myrad woman and the name *Senator Luna Liu, Myr.*

Yang tapped a button on the screen. "Hello Mother, it's Yang. I've got my friends here for the interview."

The door opened. Inside, two people sat in chairs close to each other on the near side of the desk. The woman matched the picture, and the man was someone Critch knew all too well. By some miracle, he held himself back from running in and stabbing a knife through Heid's eyes right then and there.

The woman motioned them in. "Come, come. Yang, how was your geocaching trip?"

Yang stepped in first. Critch and the others followed. Critch felt a step closer to retribution when the door closed behind them.

Yang shrugged. "I set up a new cache that I'm calling the Nutcracker."

"Yang! Watch your language," she scolded.

"I don't mean it that way," Yang said quickly. "I placed the cache in a grove of nut trees. The cache is hidden inside a case that looks like a walnut shell. They have to 'break' the shell to get to the cache."

"Well, I think you could've come up with a better name for it, but we'll talk about that later," she said. "It's your lucky day. Yang, I don't believe you've met Senator Heid before."

Yang gave a very good fanboy expression. "Senator, it's an honor."

Heid pushed to his feet. "It's a pleasure to meet the son of a woman I have the utmost respect for." He shook Yang's hand and then turned to the rest of the group. "And who are your friends?"

Luna replied first. "These are Yang's classmates. They're here to interview me for class." She smirked. "They're all hoping that if they sweet-talk me, they'll get put on the intern lottery shortlist for next year's Parliament session."

Heid smiled. "I wish you all the best." He looked down at his wrist comm. "I have work to do, but I have time to take a question if you choose.

"I've got one," Critch said.

Heid cocked his head to the side. "Your voice is familiar. Have we met before?"

"Yes. On Alluvia."

"I apologize, I don't remember. I meet a lot of people—it's a part of the job. Now, what's your question?"

Critch took a step closer. There was no sense in wasting time. "How many people have you killed?"

"What?"

That was the signal. Birk lunged and grabbed Heid's left arm to prevent the man from placing an emergency call via his wrist comm.

Critch pulled out his blaster and leveled it on Heid. Birk wrapped Heid's comm with a blocker before using a tool to detach it from the man's arm.

Heid looked at Critch, then spoke to Luna. "What do they have on you to turn on a fellow senator, Luna?"

"They have nothing on me," she replied. "I'm doing this for Gaia Welden."

He frowned. "Gaia Welden? What in the world does she have to do with me? I don't understand the correlation between her and why you're allowing these hooligans to take me hostage."

Luna glared.

After a couple seconds, Heid's features relaxed as though he found something humorous. "Ah. Damn that Seda Faulk."

Finished removing the wrist comm, Birk handed it to Throttle, who placed it into a bomb-proof bag and handed it to Luna. "Hopefully, you can find some proof in there."

Luna accepted it. "I have all the proof I need." She turned back to Heid. "I see it in your eyes. You killed Gaia, and you don't even regret it."

Heid didn't respond.

Critch nodded at Heid. "Take off your clothes, Mason."

Heid's lips thinned, but he did as instructed, all the while keeping an eye on Critch. When he left on his underwear, Critch motioned to those as well. When Mason was fully naked, Ali bagged his clothes in the same type of bag and gave it also to Luna, who was busy hiding both bags in a pot and setting the plant—which, it turned out, had been planted in a much shorter planter—on top. Birk and Throttle checked him for implants. Heid scrutinized Critch. "You're not Myrad, are you?"

Critch didn't respond.

"I know you," Heid said, but it was clear he was still trying to place Critch's face.

"Found one." Throttle grinned, snapped open her knife and sliced Heid's skin near his spine.

He grunted but didn't cry out.

She pulled out a tiny device. "You were right. He had at least one tracker on him."

Critch nodded. "We'll give him a more thorough scan back on the ship. Ted…"

Ted handed Heid a shirt and a pair of pants, and he dressed promptly. Throttle and Birk slid his hands into separate restraining bags and then bonded them together.

Luna spoke next. "You are a traitor, Gabriel. Our promise as leaders is to ensure the Collective is a place where everyone can feel safe. When you killed Gaia—and who knows who else—you broke that promise. You will pay for your crimes."

Heid smiled. "How far do you think these terrorists will get with me today? You don't think someone won't notice the co-chair of Parliament being dragged out against his will?"

Luna grinned. "No, I don't think anyone will notice. Do you remember my other son, Wang? Right now, he's in the basement with a few friends of ours. They're placing charges at every support beam." She leaned closer. "You are a rot that has contaminated the whole of Parliament. Sometimes, the only way to stop a disease is to burn it out. Parliament is going to burn today, and everyone will believe you burned down with it."

"You are a fool if you believe removing me and burning down a building will make things better," Heid said before glancing at Critch and then back at her. "You've always been a stalwart defendant of keeping citizenship from the colonists. Do your new friends know that, I wonder?"

She kept a straight face. She looked from Heid to Critch, Throttle, and Birk as she spoke. "I am not a proponent of universal citizenship. As a mother, I want good lives for my sons, and I believe the Collective would fall into a depression if we don't proceed carefully." She turned back to Heid. "Yes, I may have deep philosophical differences with the torrents, but there is one thing we both agree upon. That is the criminality of your actions, Gabriel."

"Mother," Yang said. "Wang is ready, so you need to go."

She nodded, grabbed the potted plant and strode toward the door. "Be careful, Yang."

Yang smiled. "Always."

She turned back to the occupants in the room, giving Heid a final glare. She spoke to Critch. "I have a favor to ask."

Critch tilted his head.

"Leave a piece of that murderer for me."

Critch nodded. "You got it."

With that, she opened the door and exited.

When the door closed behind her, Birk and Throttle grabbed Heid and dragged him toward the door. Ted tentatively approached the senator and covered his bound hands with a jacket.

"Drake Fender, or do you still go by Critch?" Heid asked.

Critch ignored him.

"I suspected I'd see you again, but I was hoping the circumstances would be different. I admit, I'd much prefer our situations to be reversed."

"I'm sure you would," Critch said.

The floor rumbled and alarms sounded.

"There goes the north wing," Yang said.

Critch shoved Heid forward, and they exited the office, herding around the senator and rushing down the hallway. At the front, Yang guided them to an elevator. They hurried into it, with their prisoner securely in the middle and Critch holding the muzzle of his blaster in the small of Heid's back.

"Don't use the elevator. The alarm's sounded!" a young Alluvian woman called out. "Hey! Didn't you hear me?"

They ignored her, and the door shut. Yang hit a button, and the elevator descended.

"I'm surprised you didn't call out for help," Throttle said.

"If I had, she would have come running, and you'd have killed her," Heid said.

When the elevator reached the basement, the door opened.

Before them stood Wang, Luis, Miko, and three of Miko's crew members.

"It took you long enough," Yang's twin brother said in a rush. "We've got to go now."

They hustled through the vacant area to where an unloading dock door stood open and a van sat. It was gray, windowless except for the driver's compartment, and had a plumber's logo on the side. Miko's crew helped secure Heid inside, restraining Heid's feet to the floor of the van.

Miko ran his fingers across his wrist comm. "I'm blowing the systems."

Critch looked back at the basement behind them. A series of *pop-pop* explosions erupted, and small fires lit at every electrical panel in the basement.

"There," Miko said. "That should cover any vid feeds on this block."

They climbed into the van. Wang's friend, Luis drove.

Several seconds later, a massive *boom* rattled the vehicle.

"I can't believe we blew up Parliament," Yang said with wide eyes, and several voices chattered about their victory. Soon, silence blanketed the van as the repercussions fell upon everyone.

Without windows, Critch couldn't see where they were going, so he focused his gaze on Heid, who was watching him.

"I'm impressed," Heid said. "Kidnapping a senator in broad daylight is an impressive feat."

"It's amazing what can happen when citizens and colonists work together." Critch paused for a moment. "You're a smart guy, I'll give you that. You did a lot of things right, to pull off all the stunts you have. The blight, the assassinations, the riots, the war —the list goes on. When I looked at the things I knew you had a hand in, it was always one side pitted against the other. Colonists against citizens or vice versa. That's when I figured out what your weakness was. You never thought citizens and colonists could work together. Once I knew that, it was a piece of cake to walk right up the steps of Parliament and pluck you out of your own place."

"I admit, I did not see you making that move. While bombing buildings is something you have a wealth of experience in, I'm surprised you chose to add kidnapping to your list of skills. I would've expected you to kill me instead."

Critch smiled. "Oh, I'm going to kill you. I told you that when you murdered Demes. But before I kill you, you have to stand trial for your crimes. In the fringe, we have this thing called justice."

"Ah, so you have found your scapegoat; someone to represent all the problems the fringe faces. You'll try me, find me guilty, execute me, and then what? Will everything be better? You are a fool if you believe killing one man can change generations of atti-tudes and prejudices."

Critch leaned forward. "The only thing I can guarantee will be better, is that you won't be around to play your games with people's lives. Other than that, the worlds can figure out their own problems without your interference."

"You are an idealist, and certainly not a politician," Heid said.

"I'll take that as a compliment."

"You're also shortsighted if you believe citizens and colonists will work together."

Critch shrugged. "We don't have to get along. We just have to agree to the big stuff."

"We're coming up to the docks," Luis yelled back.

"So, where are you taking me?" Heid asked. When no one answered, he continued. "Somewhere in the fringe then. Perhaps Seda's new base. I was hoping to see it."

The van pulled to a stop.

Critch turned to Throttle and Birk. "I'll see you back at the RP." He held out his right hand. Birk grabbed Critch's forearm, and Critch did the same to Birk's, the colonist handshake. He then did the same with Throttle. "Good luck."

Throttle nodded. "We'll see you out there."

The back door opened to the Liu private dock. Yang handed a keycard to Throttle. "My car is in slot G3. I'll be waiting for you, so hurry back."

Throttle grinned. "Have the engines warmed up, Chirp."

Throttle and Birk jumped out and headed in a different direction from the rest of the group, which moved toward the *Liu-Liu-1* and the *Liu-Liu-2*. Yang, Ted, and Ali broke off when they reached Yang's ship.

"Be careful," Yang said. "We'll see you soon."

Critch squeezed the Myrad's shoulder and then looked across the faces of Yang, Ted, and Ali. "You did good back there. I'd go with you into battle any day."

He turned and left before they said something sappy. Miko's crew was loading Heid on board the *Liu-Liu-2*, and Critch followed them.

As soon as Heid was secured in a bed, Miko began taping black signal blocker sheets around the senator until he was completely covered, except for his face.

"All of it," Critch said.

Miko covered Heid's face, leaving the smallest slit for the man to breathe.

"We can't be too careful. Not with this one," Critch said. "At least two guarding him at any time. You go to the bridge and keep an eye out for trouble."

"You got it, boss," Miko said, and headed down the hallway. Two of Miko's crew remained as instructed. Critch took the chair across from Heid and began to peel off the blue mask. He watched Heid for any fidgeting or sign that he may be up to something.

"Did you see Gabriela's body?" Heid asked.

Critch didn't answer.

"I don't know if you'll believe me, but I loved her," Heid continued.

Still, Critch ignored him. Heid continued, clearly trying to pique Critch's temper—whether to draw attention away from subtle escape movements or entice Critch to share information, Critch didn't care.

Heid's incessant talking made for a long flight, but it was a small price to pay for catching the devil.

CHAPTER 13

THE REUNION

Smithton, Myr

YANG PULLED up to the mansion. "Are you sure you don't want me to come in? I know the Wintsels and can—"

"No," Throttle said, cutting him off. "This isn't like Parliament. People will die in there, and I don't want that on your conscience."

Yang looked relieved. "All right. I'll be back here in ten minutes."

"We'll be ready," she said.

Throttle and Birk removed their wrist comms and left them on the back seat.

Birk leaned forward, and they kissed. After they pulled back, he spoke. "Don't start the fun without me."

Throttle smiled. "Then you'd better not be late."

She stepped out of the Rosten, and Yang and Birk departed. She took slow, confident steps toward the gargantuan mansion. When Reyne and Sixx had come to this house two years earlier, they'd snuck in through an office window in the dead of night. She strolled straight up to the front door in broad daylight.

A guard stepped out as she approached the door. He was tall and broad, and built like every other guard she'd seen on Axos's payroll.

"Is Mr. Wintsel expecting you?" he asked.

"No." She leaned closer. "But trust me, he wants to see me."

The guard looked her up and down. The corners of his lips curved upward as he surmised Throttle's intent was to get up close and personal with Axos Wintsel. In a way, he was right.

"I'll see if he is available. Your name, please," he said.

Throttle smiled. "He knows me as Halit Herley."

The guard frowned before his eyes widened. He pulled out his blaster and leveled it on her.

She held out her hands. "I'm unarmed. I'm just here to talk to Axos."

The guard spoke into his wrist comm. "I have Halit Herley at Door One, asking to see Mr. Wintsel."

Within seconds, two more guards appeared. One frisked her for weapons, double-checking her leg braces hidden by her coat, since he didn't seem to know what they were, while the other two pointed their weapons at her. Finding Throttle unarmed, he grabbed her arm and pulled her inside.

Any other Myrad would call the authorities if a known torrent came to their home. Axos wouldn't call the authorities on her because he'd want to deal with her himself.

They led her through the open foyer, down a wide hallway, and into an office. Axos sat behind a large wood desk, and Qelle Delta sat on a chaise off to the side. Since the woman didn't seem to recognize Throttle, she had to assume Delta was dead, and this iteration was Qelle Copy Echo or maybe even Foxtrot by now. This one watched her intently, but leaned back all the way as though trying to make herself as small as possible.

The guard walked Throttle to the center of the room.

Axos looked to his guards. "You, stay here. You two, search the house to make sure she didn't bring any friends."

Axos scrutinized her as he pushed to his feet. He grabbed a small device off the desk that Throttle remembered well. "I see you're walking, thanks to the implant I gave you."

"It's come in handy," she said.

He approached her and ran a finger down her cheek.

She refused to take a step back, let alone cringe.

"Blue doesn't suit your features," he said.

Throttle looked around. Books lined the walls from floor to ceiling. "So, is this the room where my father killed your mother?"

Axos's lips thinned. "It is."

"Looks like things worked out pretty good for you then. You got the house. I saw several fancy cars outside. I see you've still got a Qelle lookalike around. You know, my buddy Sixx isn't too happy about you killing his wife and making all these copies of her."

He shot his hand out and grabbed Throttle by the throat. "Where is my daughter? Where's Lily!?"

Throttle choked, though just enough air got through to allow her to utter, "Safe from you."

He shoved her away. Throttle would've fallen if not for the guard behind her. The Qelle in the corner cowered.

"You will tell me," Axos said. "I can promise you that."

She lifted a brow. "Why do you think I'm here?"

Axos paused. He'd never been the smartest person, and she could watch his expressions shift as he tried to think through the reasons. When he reached his conclusion, he guffawed. "You came here to kill me."

She grinned. "Nope."

He took a step back as though trying to determine if she was lying. "No? Then, why are you here?"

When she didn't answer, his features morphed into a snarl. He pulled out the small remote control. "You will tell me." He swiped his thumb across it.

Throttle didn't collapse. He swiped again, frowning.

She cocked her head. "Did you just try to disable my spinal implant? Because that won't work. You know, I've got a rash from having a blocker taped around my waist for months. You know how irritating that is? I'm looking forward to not worrying about that damned device any longer."

He watched her in shock. "How can you be standing?"

She grabbed the silky fabric of her long jacket and pulled it to the side for him to see the braces. "Fringe technology may not be as glamorous, but it works, too."

While he looked at her legs, she pulled out a tiny detonator that had been connected to a jacket button.

He belted out a laugh. "You came here to steal this?" He held up the remote.

She shrugged. "It was one reason."

"And the other reason?"

She smiled, though there was no humor in the expression. "To take you to Lily, of course."

Confusion marred his features. Then he sneered. "Ah, I was wondering when I'd receive a ransom demand. Tell me, what will it cost for me to get my daughter back?"

"More than what you've got," Throttle said, and she pressed the detonator.

There was no explosion. Rather, the lights suddenly went out, and the hum of the mansion's air system silenced.

Axos looked around. "What happened?"

"I don't know," the guard said.

Axos snarled. "Then find out!"

The guard opened the door. Throttle heard a shot. The guard cried out. She didn't look back and instead lunged and kneed Axos in the stomach. He fell to his knees. She swung and kicked him in the head. He collapsed, unmoving.

She pulled out restraints and turned to the Qelle, who watched with wide eyes. "You're free. Get out of here."

The woman jumped to her feet, looked at the unconscious Axos. She glanced at Throttle, then stepped forward and kicked Axos in the back before taking off running.

"You got 'im?" Birk's voice came from behind her.

She finished fastening the restraints and turned to see him step over the dead guard. "Yeah. You got them?"

Birk nodded. "Seven guards down."

"Good," she said. "Help me with him."

Birk and Throttle each grabbed one of Axos's arms, and they dragged him from the office, down the hallway, and out the front door.

Yang's brand-new Rosten sat waiting for them. Birk shoved Axos into the vehicle and climbed in, followed by Throttle. Birk pulled out several sleeping aid patches and stuck them onto Axos's neck. While they wouldn't guarantee he'd stay unconscious, they'd ensure the prisoner would be too groggy to attempt an escape.

"Are we all set?" Yang asked.

"Yes, let's get back to the *Liu-Liu-1*."

Yang nodded and sped off. Yang slowed when they reached the highway. As Throttle expected, no patrols came after them. Between Axos trusting his own security forces too much and the EMP destroying all electronics in the mansion, the authorities wouldn't know something had happened until someone stopped by the house and discovered the bodies.

Working together, they emptied Axos's pockets. They left his wrist comm on since it could do him no good after getting fried by the EMP. Finished securing their prisoner, they put their wrist comms back on and checked to make sure no emergency comms had come through.

It was hard to tamp down her adrenaline and sit without fidgeting on the ride back to the dock. She turned to Birk to see his leg bouncing. They made eye contact before they came together for a rushed kiss.

After they pulled away, Birk motioned to her torso. "You don't need to wear that thing anymore, huh?"

"Oh, yeah. The EMP." She pulled up her shirt and started tearing off the blocker taped around her torso. Birk helped her tear it off her back. The tape pulled at her skin, but for the first time, she didn't mind the sting. She wadded up the tape and blocker and dropped it on the floor.

Birk frowned and touched her skin. "That looks sore."

"It's not so bad," she said and lowered her shirt. The EMP had fried her spinal implant, meaning she was now carrying a useless piece of equipment inside her. Maybe she'd take Critch up on his offer to get her a new implant, so she could walk on her own. The braces Birk had found for her worked, and right now they felt more real to her than a tiny device that shot electrical impulses into her spine.

She smiled and leaned back in the seat. Suddenly feeling in better control, she kept an eye on their prisoner for the remainder of the trip.

Entering the space dock and departing on the *Liu-Liu-1* proved to be as hassle-free as arrival had been. As they left Myr's airspace and passed through its EMP net, the *Unity* came into view.

"Shit," Throttle muttered. "Have they pinged us?"

"No," Yang said. A moment later, he added, "It's just on its usual orbital path. It's always at Myr when Parliament's in session."

"They would've heard about the bombing already," Throttle said.

"Let's hope they're focused on hunting down terrorists and not stopping Myrad ships with approved flight plans," Yang said.

Minutes felt like hours. If they'd been a colonist ship, they would've been boarded and checked. When Yang's ship moved beyond the warship and Yang made their first jump, Throttle realized how much less stress citizens had to deal with in their daily lives.

She leaned back into her seat and sighed. She only gave herself a few moments of relaxation before she turned to her wrist comm and sent a message off to Sixx.

That blue-skin you've been looking for will be waiting for you at Nova Colony. Have fun.

A moan came from behind her. Birk jogged onto the bridge. "Sleeping Beauty's awake. You got any more sleep-strips around here?"

"No. Sorry," Yang said.

"No problem." Birk turned around and left. A moment later, Throttle heard the sound of a punch, and the moaning stopped.

She turned her attention back to the black void before them. "Hey, Yang. Think I could take the controls for a bit?"

He thought for a moment. "Sure, Why not."

She grinned.

Several hours later, Throttle docked the *Liu-Liu-1* to the *Scorpia*, which was also docked to both the *Ocelot* and the *Liu-Liu-2*. The ship connected with the lightest sound of metal on metal.

"Wow," Yang said. "That was pretty good." He sounded a bit jealous.

She pushed to her feet. "Thanks. You've got a good ship here."

He smiled.

She helped Birk drag their conscious, tantrum-throwing prisoner to the lock, and they passed through the open doors and onto
the *Scorpia.*

"Ah," she said. "It's good to be home."

"It's about time," Eddy said. "It's starting to feel like a fringe
station around here."

"Prep us for launch, Eddy," Throttle said. "We'll head out to
Devil Town as soon as we hand off this dead weight." She cocked
her head at Axos.

"Wait. You're leaving me? What's going to happen to me?"
Axos demanded.

"You're handing him off?" Critch asked as he wound through
the stairs. "I thought you'd want him all for yourself."

She looked at Axos before turning back to Critch. "Sixx
needs this. I don't. Make sure Axos stays alive long enough for
Sixx to get there, okay?"

Critch gave a small nod. "I will. You're headed to Spate?"

"Yeah," Throttle said, sparing a quick glance at Birk to make
sure he was still on board with her plan. He was. She continued.
"Operation Devil's Playground is still on the table. We're going to
take back Devil Town."

CHAPTER 14

PAYBACKS

Above Ice Port, Playa

BARRETT ANDERS ANSWERED the comm to see a rather frazzled Corps General Laciam. His hair, normally perfect, looked as though he'd run his hands through it more than once.

"Corps General, I wasn't expecting to hear from you until tomorrow."

"Parliament has been bombed," Laciam said flatly. "I need the *Caliban* for the response team."

"Of course," Barrett said. "When did this bombing happen?"

"Three, no, four, hours ago."

"How many senators did we lose?"

"We're still tracking them down. Parliament was on break, so we expect minimal casualties."

Barrett frowned as he thought. Bombing a building at a time when casualties would be at a minimum seemed at odds to when a terrorist would want to bomb. "Who bombed the building?"

"Torrents, of course. Who else would do it?"

"Have they taken credit for the attack?"

"No."

"Hm," Barrett said.

"What's that supposed to mean?"

"Seda Faulk has taken credit for every major attack. This is not like him." Barrett thought for a moment. "Did you see the torrents who bombed the building? Did you see *anyone?*"

"No. But, we're still pulling the vid feeds from the surrounding area."

"You won't find anything unusual," Barrett said. "I'd lay bets it was an inside job."

Laciam guffawed. "You're saying citizens were involved?"

"I am," Barrett said without a hint of surprise. "Have any unregistered ships bypassed the EMP nets?"

"Of course not."

"Then, if this attack was made by torrents, they had, at minimum, the help of citizens to get onto Myr, to Parliament, and—likely—are already back off Myr."

"There's no record of citizens involved in terrorist activities. They boycott and protest—they have the brains to not go further."

Barrett said, "I caution against any immediate reaction until we learn why Parliament was bombed. If there was no message, no one taking credit, the bombing hides an ulterior motive. Perhaps a diversion. Have you seen increased activity taking place anywhere in the Collective?"

"Nothing," Laciam said, "And, I don't have time for your ridiculous theories. You forced our hand into war when you cozied up with torrents. Then, you let an unknown quantity of torrents escape from Playa. When this is done, not only will you face charges for your negligence, but I will also see to it that you will never command another ship."

"If by negligence, you mean that I allowed refugees to flee before bombing an enemy location, then I stand as charged," Barrett said. "Like you, I have no desire to kill innocents, even in a time of war."

"There are no innocents in war."

Barrett ignored him. "I had reason to believe the bombing of the torrent base was considered a success—even though I didn't kill hundreds of innocent colonists—since I recovered the body of Vym Patel. However, I found it curious that the body of Commandant Jed Baptiste was with her. I wonder how a man who was believed to have been killed in the Uprising ended up on a torrent base twenty-four years after his disappearance."

"Enough," Laciam said. "I didn't reach out to chat with you. You are ordered to immediately bring the *Caliban* to meet up with the *Unity* at the Space Coast."

"The Coast? That's where all known refugees have fled."

"It's also where the torrent base is. We're going to obliterate Nova Colony and finish this war."

"As you command, Corps General," Barrett said.

As soon as Laciam disconnected, Barrett leaned back. The bombing of Parliament intrigued him. It was more than a symbolic attack—there had to be more to it than that, or else someone would've taken credit already. He wondered if the bombing was meant to draw attention from something else. Laciam, the poor idiot, only thought in terms of brute force. The Corps General was ready to kill thousands for what could have been a game of smoke and mirrors.

He tapped on his comm screen to reach out to the reporter who'd interviewed him when he first became Corps General. Perhaps, together, they could do something to keep a fool from destroying the Collective while giving an adventurous reporter the story of his life.

The comm screen came to life, and a clean-cut man's visage appeared. He smiled. "Corps General—I mean, Commandant—I'm still not used to that. What can I do for you?"

Barrett returned the smile. "On the contrary, Willas. I have a lead for you."

CHAPTER 15

FINAL PREPARATIONS

New Sol, Darios

HATHA STRODE into the command room where Reyne and Sixx were currently going over the final Silent Night plans. One of her guards followed and stood behind her.

"Have you seen the news?" she asked.

"No," Reyne said, motioning for her to take a seat at his table.

"Parliament was bombed," she said. "Tell me that was your doing."

Reyne nodded. "It was. We needed to give the CUF something else to focus on rather than hunting us down." Even though Seda and Critch had done all the planning, he considered the three torrent leaders had full accountability for every major operation they undertook.

She looked at him and then laughed. "I like your style, but have you considered your fireworks could have the opposite effect? Because Willas James says that, at this very moment, Corps General Laciam is leading the *Unity* and its complement of frigates and destroyers to the Space Coast to finish off the torrent rebellion. They're now coming at you with everything they've got."

"I figured taking down Parliament would get them all fidgety."

"Hey, boss," Sixx said softly. "Hari made it."

Reyne looked out the window just as the *Razor's Edge* settled onto the ramp. He suddenly felt a little better about the plan now that she was there with the best small fighter ship they had on their team.

Hatha continued speaking. "How many refugees are at Nova Colony? If Laciam bombs it, he could kill hundreds, if not thousands."

"Not without Gabriel Heid giving the order, he won't."

She frowned. "How'd you know Senator Heid is missing? They just announced that he is believed to have been killed in the blast."

Reyne smiled. "He's not dead."

She fanned herself. "Oh, my, you are trickier than I thought." She thought for a moment before leaning forward. "But, how do you know the corps general won't attack Nova Colony?"

"Laciam is hotheaded, but I'm guessing he doesn't have the guts to take such a direct action if he learns Heid is alive and being kept there. And hopefully, that will keep the *Unity* there long enough for us to reclaim Sol Base."

She eyed him directly. "So, does that mean we're ready?"

Reyne grinned. "Tonight's the night."

▭

Vapor had been waiting for the signal. She typed her passcode to open the program. Hardly anyone used keyboards anymore, but she found them harder to hack than comm screens, which she used only for communicating with clients. Keeping herself off-grid was how she stayed alive.

The screen before her populated with thousands of lines of code. Near the bottom of the screen was a cursor. She typed:

>>EXECUTE PROGRAM CLUSTERFUCK

A second later, the code began scrolling and then disappeared from her screen. A single response appeared below it:

>>PROGRAM SENT

Several more seconds later, another message posted:

>>PROGRAM ACTIVATED

She smiled. Of all her programs, this one had been one of the most fun to write. It wasn't complicated. Rather, it was a combination of eighty-eight viruses sent via a backdoor Trojan. A simple design, yet it would take a team of techs weeks, if not months, to decouple and evict the program, one virus at a time.

She rolled her chair over to her comm screen, scrolled through her client list, and placed the call. He answered on the first chime.

"Your little warship should have its hands full in exactly eighteen minutes," she said.

"Excellent," Seda Faulk said. "The credits have been transferred to your account."

She checked a small window of her screen to verify her account. Seeing he was true to his word, she sent him the packet. "I sent you the antivirus. All you have to do it run it on any computer on board the warship, and everything will be as good as new. Pleasure doing business with you." She reached to disconnect.

"I have one more job for you, Vapor," Seda said.

She paused. "What do you need?"

"For you to take a look behind you."

Her breath caught, and she spun in her chair, only to have it stopped. A black bag went over her face. She fought to get free, but her assailant tied her hands far too quickly.

"Vapor, I know it was your program that killed Gabriela Heid," Seda said.

She froze. "It was just a job."

The next words came from the man right by her ear. "Then you'll understand that you're just a job for me, too."

With that, she felt a sharp, stinging slice across her neck. Warm wetness soaked her skin and poured down her chest. Then, the burning agony came. She sucked in a breath but couldn't find air. She reached for her throat, but her hands were still restrained. She kicked and fought for breath.

"I should warn you, Seda; Mason has sent me to kill you," she heard the man in the room say.

"Ah, I see," Seda said. "Thank you for letting me know."

They continued to speak, but a frigid darkness overtook Vapor and gelled the men's words into black ice.

CHAPTER 16

SILENT NIGHT

Sol Base, Darios

THE *LITTORIO'S* lights blinked and then went dark.

Sixx chuckled. "The bigger they are, the harder they fall."

"The warship's dead in the water," the tech confirmed.

"Let's hope it stays down," Reyne said.

"It'd be great if we could load the virus onto every CUF ship across the Collective. Then, this war would be over," Sixx said.

"I wish that were the case," Reyne said. "Even Vapor couldn't send it out to all the ships at once. Unfortunately, as soon as the CUF learns how Vapor got through their firewall, they'll have a patch loaded onto all of their ships."

Reyne sent out a ping to the wrist comms of twelve thousand torrents and two thousand resistance fighters involved in the operation. The next step began as softly as a toddler's snore. From his video feeds across the city, he watched as people bled out casually onto the streets. The scattered dromadiers performing their security walks didn't seem to notice the colonists; after all, it was in between work shifts and they wouldn't have received any warning from the *Littorio*.

It wasn't until colonists were on the streets by the thousands that the dromadiers figured out it wasn't another, ordinary evening. Reyne scanned the feeds to see pairs of dromadiers raising their blasters and yelling at the crowds to disperse. Fortunately, none had fired yet. The fighters weren't supposed to reveal their weapons until the dromadiers drew first blood. That way, Hatha would have a clean video of what looked to be a peaceful boycott ending in the CUF bringing violence. Reyne knew the video wouldn't change the outcome of the war, but videos had the power to create doubt in the minds of citizens over who was really in the right. And when it came to peace negotiations, the more support the fringe had, the better.

Reyne hoped the dromadiers wouldn't fire upon a crowd, but he knew better. Something would always happen when someone with a twitchy trigger finger found himself in a stressful situation. It was as guaranteed as finding a card game in Devil Town.

The plan was as straightforward as possible. Reyne couldn't afford complex maneuvers when working with fourteen thousand relatively inexperienced fighters who were at as much risk from friendly fire as from the CUF.

The *Littorio* would be out of action as it dealt with a virus across all its systems, which would also prevent it from launching its gunships. That left four destroyers; however, Reyne assumed they would be impacted to some extent by the virus by being linked to the warship. How badly impacted waited to be seen.

He was confident they could take Sol Base from the ground. A few dozen dromadiers against a horde of armed colonists made that result inevitable. Holding on to Sol Base was another story.

The sky was an uneven match, heavily tilted in the CUF's favor. The destroyers carried many times the armament. A single shot could annihilate a ship, while a destroyer could take dozens of critical hits. What helped the specters, however, was the fact that they were small and nimble. They could change direction in seconds, while destroyers were slow and moved like icebergs.

Reyne tapped the comm channel. "Specters, you have a green light. Go sting some CUF ass."

Reyne watched his video feed. Seconds later, one dozen dots appeared over the horizon and quickly approached the colony. When he could make out the individual shapes, the ships changed direction and shot upward toward the complement of CUF ships sitting above Sol Base.

A destroyer fired photon blasts. Reyne swallowed. "Damn. I was hoping the virus would've taken out the destroyers' weapons systems."

"The specters can hold their own as long as that warship is out of commission," Sixx said from the chair next to Reyne's.

"Let's just hope they can hold their own long enough for that CUF commandant to surrender." That was the critical unknown piece to the operation: the success of the operation depended on if and when the CUF commandant would surrender. Otherwise, it was simply a matter of who won the battle in the air.

"First shot's been fired on the ground. Unfortunately, it looks like we may have fired first." Sixx pointed to a feed in the lower left of the screen where lights of blaster fire sparkled, and the dromadiers fell. When the firing stopped, several colonists also lay on the ground.

Reyne's jaw tightened. "We knew that was a risk. I guess that means we won't be using that video."

Hatha, who'd been sitting quietly while watching the screens, spoke. "I hope we have at least one good feed to use. The Darions work very hard at keeping a reputation of being pacifists."

"You've got your video," Sixx said, pointing to another feed. "Another shot fired near the station. Clearly droms this time, and the crowd hasn't fired back." He winced as the crowd swarmed the pair of dromadiers. "Though the droms may not survive."

"That story is easy enough to spin," Hatha said. "Send me the feed, and I'll get it sent out to all the news outlets within the hour."

"Let's hope they bite."

"They'll see that it's unaltered video. They'll show it. What they report in regard to it, we have no control over."

"It'd be nice to still have that hacker around, so we could broadcast it ourselves," Sixx said.

Reyne nodded. "But, I'd rather have her out of the picture." There was only one hacker who had the capabilities to broadcast across all the Collective channels, and it was the same hacker who could get a virus loaded onto CUF systems without getting noticed. Unfortunately, it was also the same hacker who'd written the program that caused Gabriela Heid's tablet to explode, killing her. Once the hacker coded that particular program, she'd switched from a hacker to an assassin, and Reyne understood Seda's decision to have her killed... by his own assassin, ironically.

The tech managing all the feeds spoke up. "Stationmaster Satine, I've sent the video to your second account."

"Thank you, Sammy," she said and stood. "I'll see you all within the hour. Sammy, keep me apprised in the meantime."

Hatha departed, leaving the trio in the room.

Sixx looked at Sammy. "Did you just call her, 'stationmaster'?"

Sammy nodded. "Yeah. We all do. Who else is right for the job?"

Sixx shrugged. "True. I suppose we no longer have to wait for Parliament to approve our stationmasters anymore. There's nothing stopping the colonies from doing it themselves."

"Exactly." Sammy winced at the screen. "Ouch. That was a nasty hit."

Reyne analyzed the battle taking place above through the feeds coming from each ship.

"Our team in the skies is taking a beating," Sixx said. "*Crazy's Coral's* left engine is spitting juice. *Skye Rider* has broken off and is limping back to the dock."

"All the droms on the ground have either surrendered or been killed," Sammy said.

"Good," Reyne said. "Broadcast over all speakers that all prisoners are to be brought to the station and that we have control of the ground."

It became clear when the news was made, because all the ground feeds showed people cheering. He turned his attention back to the feeds of the battle taking place in the sky. One of the destroyers had a gaping hole where one engine was before. The *Razor's Edge* made a strafing run down the side, while the *Maelstrom* fired its cannon at the hole. An explosion began at the destroyer's back, blowing its way forward and obliterating the ship into a debris field.

"Yeah!" Sixx yelled. "One down, three to go!"

"Marshal," Sammy said. "One of the prisoners is receiving comms from the commandant, who wants to get in touch with you."

Reyne nodded, having expected that. "Bring the prisoner in here." With the virus wiping out the warship's comms, among everything else, the commandant would've been able to communicate with his teams via wrist comms only.

Sammy's eyes widened. "Into the command room? Is that safe?"

"It's the only way to keep an eye on the sky to make sure the officer's not trying diversionary tactics. Besides, Sixx here will keep an eye on the drom."

Sixx grinned. "It'll be my pleasure." His grin fell. "Aw, damn it. The *Coral* just checked out."

Reyne turned back to the screen to see *Crazy's Coral* broken into halves. He'd met the crew, and shared drinks with its captain, Ten Speed, on more than one occasion. "Were there any escape pods?"

"No," Sammy said quietly.

The remaining destroyers were lining up into an arrow point formation. "They're getting ready for a coordinated assault. Tell the specters to go into stealth if they've still got enough juice. That way, the destroyers will have to manually lock on."

The door opened, and two of Hatha's hired guns stepped inside with a bloodied soldier between them. Sixx came to attention and held a blaster.

The dromadier stood straight, so Reyne assumed he wasn't suffering from broken bones or internal injuries, though it was difficult to assess injuries through the dark navy suit. He glanced at the man's patches. An Alluvian, tech level, so likely young, but it was hard to tell through the blood streaking his face.

"This drom is in contact with the guy in charge up there," one of the guards said.

"Good," Reyne said and turned to the soldier.

"*Blue Jay*'s been hit," Sammy said.

Reyne turned to the screen to see the smallest of the specters lit up from inside. He winced. On board fires were the worst way to go. He frowned as the ship turned and reentered the battle. Somehow, someone was still able to fly that thing. The ship increased speed as it headed directly at a destroyer. The CUF ship fired, but not in time. *Blue Jay* screamed past the destroyer's nose and crashed into the bridge. The destroyer listed and then broke off from formation.

"*Blue Jay*'s gone, but she took a destroyer with her," Sammy said. "That leaves two destroyers against ten specters."

"They'll hold their own just fine," Sixx said, and Reyne knew what his friend meant. As long as the destroyers were distracted, they couldn't fire at the ground, where they could slaughter a hundred with a single, searing photon blast.

Reyne turned to the dromadier. "Please put your commandant online."

The man did as instructed. "Sir, they want to talk with you." He held out his wrist comm.

"This is Commandant Corll of the CUF *Littorio*. To whom am I speaking?"

Reyne pointed to a comm screen sitting several feet away from the computers on which they'd been watching the battle. "Send the comm to that screen so I can see who I'm talking to."

The soldier pointed his wrist comm to the screen and tapped to link the two devices.

Reyne stood in front of the screen. The Alluvian officer was young, angry, and, by the sweat glistening on his face, in way over his head. "Hello, Commandant. I'm Marshal Aramis Reyne of the Fringe Liberation Campaign. We have taken your ground forces, and your ship is dead in the water. That leaves two of your destroyers—"

"We just took down another destroyer!" Sammy said with a *whoop*.

"That leaves a single destroyer to fend off a torrent fleet," Reyne corrected. "I'm here to offer you terms of surrender."

"I will not surrender to you," Corll replied. "Your victory over the ground is temporary. I don't know how you managed to get a virus on board the *Littorio*, but we have rebooted the systems and will rain hellfire on you if you do not surrender."

Reyne sneered and called what he hoped to be a bluff. "Rebooting the systems will do no good. Your ship is dead, and it will remain dead long after you run out of air to breathe. So, I give you terms. Surrender to the conscripts on board your ship, and you and all citizens will be brought down to the surface, where you'll be placed in holding cells until peace is negotiated with Parliament. And, if any conscripts are listening who are on board the remaining destroyer, this message is for you: If you place the colonies' independence in your best interest, we promise you safety and protection."

Corll laughed. "Conscripts are as much a part of the Forces as citizens are. They will not turn—" He froze as he looked away from the screen.

The video on the screen jiggled as though Corll's arm had been grabbed. A woman's face appeared via the commandant's wrist comm. "This is Chaser Shauna Fields. I'm the senior-most conscript on board the *Littorio*. I have relieved Commandant Corll of his command, and we are in process of taking the ship now."

"You will be shot for this," Corll said offscreen, and the screen shook.

He heard Corll grunt, and the screen became steady again. Fields returned.

"The *Littorio*'s prior captain was more likeable," Reyne said.

"Yes, he was," Fields said. "I want you to know that we are in communication with our compatriots on the *Houston*. They're hoping to negotiate, but the captain is still in control. We request that you are true to your word and not let us die up here."

"Good work, Chaser Fields," Reyne said. "You have my word. Colonists are safe."

"Call me Shauna," she said. "I guess since I just committed mutiny against my captain, I no longer have that title."

Reyne glanced at Sammy. "Send this comm screen number to Corll's wrist comm." He turned back to Shauna. "Pull my comm screen code so you can reach me. Send me your wrist comm code. That way, we no longer have to go through a middle man."

He heard Corll moan, and he wondered what had happened to the commandant.

Reyne continued. "Notify me as soon as you have both ships fully under your control. I'll then apprise you of next steps."

Shauna nodded. "I will."

The screen went blank.

"The destroyer's stopped firing," Sammy said.

"That means something's happening on board," Reyne said. "How are the specters looking?"

"Not great," Sammy said. "*Winter Wind* and *Razor's Edge* are the only two who haven't taken a hit. The others are still in the field, but some are showing structural damage."

"Get the transports in the air. As soon as that destroyer stands down, get the damaged specters out of there, starting with the ones most at risk of breaking apart. If they can't fly out on their own, get a transport out there to pick up their crew."

The comm screen chimed, and Reyne tapped it to see Shauna's face.

"The *Littorio* is fully under colonist control," she said. "Captain Singh of the *Houston* willingly surrenders his ship and crew in exchange for their safety."

"The safety of his crew is promised as long as they do as instructed. They are to leave their weapons on the ship and take transports down to the docks. There, they will be met by Darion security forces. Citizens will be processed into a holding facility. We have housing available for all colonists who voluntarily refuse their CUF service."

"How about us on board the *Littorio*, Marshal? Our transports are dead, and we only have enough air for four days."

"I'm sending transports up to you. Same deal goes to your crew. You and I will debrief after you land. I've got something for you to get that warship back online and a couple thousand extra crew members—that is, if you want to use it to stand up against the CUF."

She grinned. "Of course I do. See you on the ground."

Reyne sighed. The operation could've gone sideways in so many different ways, though he knew hundreds of lives were lost.

"You haven't won," the dromadier said. "This was just one battle. You can't beat us. We have the ships and the guns and the money to keep them coming at you."

Reyne looked at the young man, who he realized represented the CUF's mindset pretty well. Confident, intelligent, but naïve.

"Perhaps," Reyne said. "But you're lacking the one thing the fringe has through and through. Resilience."

CHAPTER 17

CHESS GAMES

Nova Colony within the Space Coast asteroid belt

SEDA STEPPED out of the airlock along with his guards, Tax and Corbin, to find Critch waiting for him in a flight suit, with only his face shield open.

"You're late," Critch said.

"I've been busy coordinating activities," Seda said, pulling off his own helmet. "There's more negotiating and hand-holding involved in running a war than I ever imagined."

Critch grunted. "I'm glad you're handling that end, but if you'd delayed much longer, you would've found half of the CUF armada lined up along the Coast, ready to welcome you into a prison cell."

"I certainly hope it doesn't come to that, assuming our guest in our own prison cells is alive and well."

"He's alive," Critch said. "I've got a ride leaving in ten minutes to bring me to Terra. Try not to kill him until I get back."

"Trust me, he's worth far more to us alive. He started the war; I'm planning on using him to help end it."

Critch chuckled and patted Seda's shoulder. "Good luck with that." He motioned to the woman standing by him. "This is Layla. She'll show you around and take care of you while you're here. You can trust her with your life."

With that, Critch closed his face shield, stepped around Seda into the airlock, and disappeared behind the closing door.

"So, you're Seda Faulk," Layla mused. "I'm impressed. You're even more handsome in person."

He looked at her. She wore a dress, if it could even be called that. Her boots covered more skin than the band of tight clothing around her torso. He could imagine that Critch's warped sense of humor had found hiring a prostitute for Seda funny.

"Thank you, I suppose." He gestured to the pair of men at his back. "This is Tax, and this is Corbin. They go wherever I go."

"Mm," she said. "Hello, fellas. I want to go wherever you go, too." She turned back to Seda. "So where would you like to go first?"

"I'm sure I can find my way around. Can you point me in the right direction to where the prisoners are kept?"

She grabbed his right arm and looped her hand through, tugging them closer together. He noticed his men tense, but neither pulled her away from him.

She grinned. "I'll do you one better. I'll show you."

Her brow furrowed, and she squeezed his arm. "Synthetic?"

He nodded. "I lost it just below the shoulder."

She cocked her head. "It fits you nicely." Then, she gently pulled him forward. As she led him through the wide tunnel, he noticed people watching him. He'd been hidden away for so long, the sudden attention was almost unnerving.

"Wow," Layla began. "This might be the first time they aren't looking at me." She shrugged. "It's not every day people see our fearless leader."

"I'm not the only leader, and I can assure you, I'm certainly not fearless."

She turned them down a slightly smaller tunnel. Seda had the sensation that they were descending, but that was more dependent on where the electromagnetic gravity system was placed than from what was up or down.

"Doesn't matter what you think. You're the guy who signed the cease-fire. And, even more important, Critch seems to listen to you."

"I don't believe Critch listens to anyone."

She shrugged. "Critch practically owns Nova Colony. Just about everyone here, myself included, works for him. He wouldn't have gotten that far if he wasn't a bit hardheaded. But I've seen him do what you asked, even if he wasn't happy about it."

"I've never seen him happy about anything," Seda said.

She gave a small smile. "I heard he used to be happy, a long time ago. But I guess that's what the Collective does to a colonist over time."

She turned, and the next tunnel definitely gave the feeling that they were descending into the bowels of the asteroid. The stone walls were rougher, and there were fewer lights and people.

"You said you work for Critch. What do you do?" Seda asked.

Corbin snickered behind him.

"I work at the Uneven Bar," Layla said, unbothered.

"Ah, so you're a... bartender?"

Corbin snickered louder.

She looked up at him with a sideways smile. "I think we both know I'm not a bartender."

He stumbled awkwardly. "Of course. Sorry I asked."

"It's honest work." She pulled away and stopped. "Listen, if you'd rather have someone else—"

"No," Seda cut in. "You're fine. It's just—"

Her brows rose. "That you're not used to talking when you're with a whore?"

"No, it's not that." He frowned. As president of several companies, he'd always had to worry about public relations. "Honestly, I don't think I've ever met one."

She laughed. "Oh, I'm sure you have. You just didn't know it."

"Yeah," Corbin said behind him. "He's met a few."

She smiled as she looped her hand through his arm again, and they continued their walk.

Even though he was Terran and had spent plenty of time in its underground tunnels, he was thoroughly lost in the asteroid. He found Layla's warm closeness comforting. He couldn't remember the last time he'd been touched by a woman.

"We're here," Layla said. She unhooked herself from Seda and led the way to a dead-end tunnel lined with cells. Three guards sat at equal intervals. She kept walking until they reached the very last cell.

This one had a much smaller window than the others, and a guard sat just outside the door. The guard stood as they approached. "Hey, Layla. How're you doing?"

"Doing good, Drew," she said. "Though, we'd all be doing better if that guy in there wasn't breathing."

Seda glanced down at her to see her scowling.

"I wanted to slice his neck, but Critch wouldn't let me."

He frowned. "You know him?"

"Rumor is he killed Captain Heid. She was the one who came to our rescue when the CUF tried to suffocate us, so he has a bundle of enemies around here." She turned back to the guard. "Hey, Drew, Seda's here to chat with the prisoner."

"Sure." The man, easily in his fifties, turned around and entered a passcode on the keypad near the door. It unlocked and then opened outward.

Layla remained by the door. Seda stepped inside, with Tax at his side. Corbin stood in the open doorway. Seda would've preferred to speak with Heid alone, but he knew his guards would never allow him to take such a risk.

Gabriel Heid pushed off the bed and to his feet.

"Ah, if Aeronaut hasn't just chosen to grace me with his presence." Heid then took in Seda's protectors. "I'm surprised to see you without Mechanic. Did one of my people kill her?"

Seda's gaze narrowed. Heid was purposely using Founder names, likely to throw off the guards. What Heid didn't realize was that Tax and Corbin knew all of Seda's secrets already, and he was hoping Layla wouldn't become a wild card. "*Hari* is alive and well. She's on her way back from Darios." He lifted a brow. "Oh. Haven't you heard? We've retaken Sol Base."

Any hint of humor drained from Heid's face before he recomposed himself. "Impressive feat. I had not expected you to focus your efforts there after the population had been wiped out. It seemed an unnecessary use of your limited resources."

Seda took a step closer. "I admit, you lined up your moves nicely. You understand the size of the CUF armada and what it's capable of—and not capable of. You took Ice Port and Sol Base out of the picture early with hard strikes. But you spread the Forces too thin by having them simultaneously take Devil Town and Rebus Station while still monitoring Sol Base."

Heid shrugged. "I had to move quickly or else risk losing favor in Parliament. If Parliament fails, everything fails." Heid began to pace slowly back and forth. "You see, the Collective has grown too diverse to function as a cohesive unit. Like an old forest, it's become stagnant. In much the same way a forest fire helps life thrive after the fire, the Collective needs a fire of its own to reset so that it may grow better than before."

Seda guffawed. "Don't pretend that you're doing this for the benefit of the Collective. Diversity isn't the Collective's problem.

It's your problem. Even with all the games you played through the Founders, there have become too many variables for you to manage. You need the forest fire so you can control everything again."

"You talk like I'm trying to destroy the colonies."

"The numbers speak for themselves. How many tens of thousands of colonists have you killed so far?"

Heid waved him off. "I do not dislike the colonies. After all, they're crucial for the Collective to thrive. Myr and Alluvia have barely enough resources to support themselves, let alone expansion."

Seda's gaze tightened on the prisoner. "If that's the case, why did you not guide Parliament to recognize the colonies as equal states within the Collective?"

"It wouldn't work. Two citizen worlds bring a perfect balance, like ying and yang, to the Collective—equal in all ways. If the colonies were allowed the same status, the Collective would no longer be two worlds working collaboratively but instead two worlds at odds against the four newcomers. Simple mathematics shows that everything would fall out of balance. If the four colonies took the majority in Parliament, all the history and progress made to date would be halted, as the newcomers lack the political understanding and history that comes from generations of progress. At best, there'd be political deadlock; at worst, there'd be new wars. Every outcome would result in the fall of the Collective."

Seda sneered. "You'll get to keep your precious balance between two worlds, because soon, the colonies will have their independence. They'll form their own government structures however they see fit, and the Collective will need to negotiate trade with them."

Heid paused and faced Seda. "You haven't won the war yet.

You may have Sol Base, but it will be a short-lived victory. We both know the CUF has larger cannons."

Seda held up a finger. "Ah, but you can't take Sol Base by force. That's why you used the blight the first time. You can't risk damaging the docks or else you'll have no way of transporting all that food Alluvia and Myr need to survive. So, now the CUF is forced to try to gain Sol Base back using dromadiers on the ground, and colonists outnumber them a hundred to one. You no longer have a brief war."

"The longer the war lasts, the greater the damage on *both* sides," Heid cautioned.

"Citizens will quickly lose the taste for war when their bellies are empty," Seda said. "More important, now that we have you, they'll lose their appetites even faster."

"You misjudge my value if you believe taking me brings you closer to independence."

"I do believe that," Seda said. "True, we needed Sol Base to make Myr and Alluvia cry out for peace. But taking you away from the game table leaves Laciam floundering and Etzel in charge of Parliament. From what I hear, Etzel desires peace more than anything, perhaps more than holding the Collective together."

Heid glared.

Seda lowered his chin. "Check and mate."

Heid took a step closer. "First, you betrayed the Founders. Then, you betrayed the Collective. If the Collective falls, *you* are responsible for all that's lost."

Seda's expression grew harder. "I'll gladly take that responsibility."

Heid cocked his head. "Mariner died as a result of your betrayal. Do you know how she died?"

Inside, Seda seethed, but he'd known Heid would take a hit at his heart and was prepared for it. "No. My wife died because you killed her. Just as your daughter died because you killed her. Neither of their deaths served a greater good, nor did they right a wrong. Their deaths only served to nurture your own psychosis."

Seda turned, then paused. "And the Collective is falling because of your actions. You are responsible for that."

"I exist to help the Collective!" Heid yelled.

Seda left the cell, knowing his guards would protect him should Heid try to attack from behind. To Seda's surprise, Heid didn't attack, and the door closed, keeping the prisoner within his cell.

Seda took a breath, finding some amount of satisfaction in making Heid lose his temper. He gave each of his guards a thankful nod before turning to Layla.

She was leaning against the wall, cleaning her fingernails with a long, narrow blade.

He frowned, looking at her outfit. "Where'd that come from?"

Her lips curved upward. "You really want to know?"

He clamped his mouth shut.

"So... did you get what you need from him?"

"I needed to see him alive and feel confident that he'll stay that way, so the answer is yes."

"Where to now?" Layla asked.

"Now, we see about turning a warship away from the Coast." He held out his arm for her to loop her hand through. She slid the knife into her boot and placed her hand around his elbow.

"I like the sound of that."

▭

The *Unity* reached the edge of the Space Coast five hours later. By then, Seda had dispatched every civilian ship in a fifty-sector radius to fly out to meet the warship. Each of the civilian ships sent messages that they flew under flags of truce. Even so, it was a gamble Seda did not like taking.

When Seda had proposed his plan to all the civilian captains, every single one had volunteered to travel out to the *Unity*, even though their ships had no weapons of their own. Their job was to give the CUF a peaceful show of resistance, i.e., if the CUF was going to bomb Nova Colony, they'd need to bomb over one hundred white flag-flying civilian ships as well.

Seda stood in Nova Colony's command room, which he'd learned was actually Critch's command room, connected to Critch's residence, where Seda would be staying. He watched the blips form up on the screen along the outside edge of the asteroid belt. Blue for all the civilian ships, red for the *Unity*, two frigates, and six destroyers.

He was about to have the tech ping the warship when he noticed something. He pointed at a yellow dot. "Whose ship is that?"

"Yellow is usually either humanitarian or press access." The tech tapped it and scrolled through its details. "Yup. Press. It belongs to DZ-Five News."

Seda stared at it for a moment, rubbing his chin. He could think of only two reasons why the news would be on hand for a military operation. Either the CUF had leaked information to have the operation broadcast, or some reporter had sniffed out a story and tagged along.

He lowered his hand. "Ping them."

The tech looked back. "You want me to ping DZ-Five? They report Collective news, not ours."

"Remember Lina Tao? They're not all brainwashed by the Collective. Now, ping that ship."

The tech seemed dubious but sent a ping to the ship, anyway.

Moments later, the tech comm chimed. He shrugged, surprised. "They've accepted our request to chat."

"Answer it," Seda said.

The face of Willas James appeared on screen. He wasn't just any reporter; he was one of the most famous reporters in the system, known for showing up on the most dangerous scenes.

"This is Willas James of DZ-Five News. I have press access to the full Collective system, and I intend to report the news. To whom am I speaking?"

Seda motioned for the tech to move.

The tech's eyes widened, and he spoke in a hurried whisper. "No one can know you're here. If the CUF knows you're at Nova Colony, they'll bomb—"

"Let me handle this," Seda said. He took the tech's seat to place himself in front of the screen. He went to video.

The reporter's brows lifted and his jaw loosened.

"I'm Seda Faulk of the Fringe Liberation Campaign. What brings you out this far, Citizen James?"

The reporter's features smoothed. "I'm here to report a story. I heard the *Unity* was headed out this way to possibly bomb Nova Colony. Seeing you, now I understand why."

"Laciam doesn't know I'm here, so I can assure you I'm not the reason," Seda said. "He's come here to bomb a colony full of refugees in retaliation for the bombing of Parliament. This is just a revenge stop for him before he heads to Darios to face off against the Darions, who are now back in control of their world."

Willas frowned. "I saw the video of the Sol Base boycotts, but no one said anything about losing the planet. What do you mean the Darions are now in control of Darios?"

Seda cocked his head. He had no doubt the entire conversation was being recorded and so he stated his words carefully. "I see Corps General Laciam is withholding information from the press. Three days ago, torrent forces led by Marshal Aramis Reyne took control of Sol Base as well as the warship *Littorio*. Casualties totaled sixty-four. Commandant Corll and the citizen dromadiers who report to him are currently in custody on Sol Base. They will be released, unharmed, upon Parliament's acceptance of the cease-fire signed by Corps General Barrett Anders and myself. This is what I relayed to both Maximus Laciam and Senator Etzel on multiple occasions, and once again after reclaiming Sol Base."

Willas looked blankly ahead for a moment, clearly upset that whatever deals he had worked out with officers, senators, or both, had been reneged. Willas looked directly at Seda. "You are currently an enemy of the state. I hope you understand why I can't take your words as truth, but I will perform my due diligence and verify if what you've said is accurate. If Sol Base has fallen, there will be many upset citizens wondering how soon the food will run out."

"We don't intend to cut off the food supply," Seda said. "However, I have no control over Laciam's phase cannons should he attempt to re-take Sol Base by force. If citizens starve, it will be by the CUF's doing."

"Did you reach out to me today to tell me about Sol Base?"

"No," Seda said. "I reached out to you to see if you could get a message out. Should Corps General Laciam invade the Space Coast, and fire on Nova Colony, he will kill Senator Gabriel Heid as well as six thousand refugees—along with a half dozen torrents."

Willas frowned. "Senator Heid was killed in the bombing of Parliament, for which I was led to believe you were responsible."

"The bombing was a joint operation, by citizens and colonists, to destroy a building that represented oppression to the majority of the Collective. And Senator Heid is alive and currently sitting in a prison cell here on Nova Colony. He was arrested for the murder of Citizen Gaia Welden, Commandant Gabriela Heid, and over seventy thousand colonists on Sol Base. Here, he will stand trial for his crimes." When Willas opened his mouth to speak, Seda continued. "I have proof of his crimes and can share that with you should we come to a mutually beneficial agreement to work together. The only fact you need to know right now is that Senator Heid is in my custody on Nova Colony. I'm sending over a video now to give you the proof you need."

Willas looked away from the screen for several seconds as he examined the footage of Heid sitting in his prison cell. He returned focus to the comm screen. "I'll get the message out."

"You can save six thousand lives today," Seda said.

"I'm not picking sides," Willas said. "I report the news as I see it."

"Of course," Seda answered.

Willas lifted his chin. "If there are going to be talks between you and the CUF or Parliament, I want to know."

Seda thought for a moment. "Consider it done. Send your personal comm address."

"Sent. Plus, grant me an exclusive story with you. You're the face of the rebellion. Give me your side of the story."

Seda smirked. This man was a reporter through and through. "If I'm alive after today, I'll give you an exclusive interview, Citizen James."

He smiled. "Call me Willas."

"You can call me Seda." He disconnected the comm.

"We should get you off this asteroid," Tax said from behind him.

"I'm not leaving," Seda said. "If I leave, it will look like I think I'm more important than any other colonist here. What would that inspire? No, I'm a colonist, and I'm staying with my fellow colonists through thick and thin."

"You're a hardheaded bastard," Corbin mumbled.

Seda leaned back. "Turn on the news. Let's see if DZ-Five will still report the news, or if it's smothered."

Twenty-two tense minutes later, Seda watched Willas James

report that Senator Heid was alive and being held at Nova Colony, and that Corps General Laciam was sitting outside the Coast instead of going to Sol Base, as the latter had fallen to rebels three days ago.

"He never mentioned you," Tax said.

"He's a better reporter than I thought," Seda said. "With only Heid and refugees at Nova Colony, it would reflect very poorly on Laciam should he attack. If I was known to be here, then there would be some in favor of attacking, regardless of the casualties."

"Do you think he's on our side?" Tax asked.

"Willas James is on his own side," Seda said.

"Should we relocate Heid?" Corbin asked. "They'll likely send in teams to rescue him."

"I don't think they will," Seda said. "Heid has dirt on so many people they may hope he stays here for a very long time."

"The *Unity* is moving," the tech exclaimed.

Seda leaned forward. The red blips on the screen were backing away from the Coast and building a jump formation. Three minutes later, the blips disappeared.

Cheers erupted.

Seda hit the intercom for the entire asteroid and all the civilian ships. "The CUF has decided not to play with us today. They've bugged out. We're safe for now. Thank you for your help, and you can return to whatever you were doing before we had to stand up to the schoolyard bully."

Seda leaned back and let out a deep breath. They'd gotten lucky. He pushed to his feet and clasped the tech's shoulder. "Warn Reyne that the *Unity* is on its way."

As the room emptied, Corbin moved to the bar and poured four drinks, bringing one back to Seda and handing the others to Tax and Layla. They clinked their glasses, and Seda savored the drink.

"Critch has the good stuff," Tax said.

The four sat around and enjoyed each other's company after the stressful experience of nearly getting bombed into oblivion. As time passed, Tax checked out Critch's rooms to make sure they were safe. After several minutes, he popped his head through the doorway. "All clear."

Seda stood. "I'm ready to call it a night."

Layla ran a hand softly down his left arm and gave him a hooded look. "Need help getting tucked in?"

He glanced at the door. A smile formed on his face. "I might." And he meant it.

CHAPTER 18

FRAYED STANDOFF

Sol Base, Darios

"MARSHAL, the *Unity* and its complement has just emerged from jump and is less than three hours out. Laciam has two frigates and three destroyers more than us, plus a lot more trained dromadiers," Shauna reported from the *Littorio*.

In the Sol Base command room, Reyne shot a glance at Sixx and Sammy before turning back to the screen. "Be ready to jump if they start shooting. The same goes for the *Houston*. If they attack, they're going to take Sol Base, but at least we can prevent them from getting their warship and destroyer back."

She nodded. "We'll be ready."

"Until he shows aggression, give him no reason to believe that the *Littorio* and the *Houston* aren't dead in the black. The last thing we want is a fight. Our goal is to negotiate an armistice."

She lifted a brow. "You haven't met Corps General Laciam yet, have you?"

Reyne scowled. "No. I heard he has an over-abundance of confidence."

She laughed. "You just described every citizen I've ever met."

"He may be hotheaded, but he's got to be smart to be the position he's in. I'm counting on him knowing what's best for the Collective and not come in shooting."

"Good luck with that," she said.

Reyne disconnected the comm.

"You really think they'll jump if Sol Base is fired upon?" Sixx asked.

"I have no idea," Reyne replied. "They have a bone to pick with the CUF, just like we do. Whether they stay and fight or run to fight another day... I just don't know what they'll do."

Hatha entered the room with Tully at her side. "I heard the *Unity* has reached our sector."

"It has, along with a full complement of frigates and destroyers," Reyne said. "We have three hours tops before they get here. That's assuming they're coming in close to talk and not just fire on us as soon as they reach firing range."

She frowned. "I'd like to think they wouldn't bomb their own food supply. Speaking of which, because of the CUF blockade, I've grounded all Alluvian and Myr transports in the docks."

"There's no blockade yet," Reyne said.

"I may have been a couple hours premature on my message; however, we both know there will be a blockade as soon as the *Unity* arrives."

"I bet the transport drivers are none too happy sitting in the middle of the war's hotbed," Sixx chimed in.

"They'll like it less if the food starts to rot in their cargo holds," Hatha said before turning back to Reyne. "I've already notified my brokers on both Alluvia and Myr that their current shipments are delayed due to the CUF's blockade, and they won't see another shipment until the transports can depart without being shot or seized."

Reyne spoke. "Having empty shelves in the grocery stores will certainly inspire citizens to call their senators and demand them to negotiate. Since you've never been linked to the torrents, you'll have a better chance at talking with Laciam. Are you good with that?"

"Of course."

"Stationmaster, Marshal, there's a ship that emerged from jump just outside our airspace."

"Is it CUF?" Reyne asked.

"No. It's broadcasting media codes." He ran his hands over the screen. "The captain says they're transporting Willas James of DZ-Five News, and he's requesting clearance to land under the Fair News and Reporting Act."

"Excellent. Let him land," Hatha said.

"Hold on," Reyne said. "Could it be a trap? Why would the press want to be on the ground rather than on board the *Unity* where it's much safer?"

"I don't know, and I don't care," Hatha said. "Having the Collective's news channel down here, on the ground, means that if the *Unity* fires upon us, everyone in the system will see."

"That's assuming he's not coming down here to put the Collective spin on what's happening here. Him emerging from jump right after the *Unity* can't be a coincidence. Don't trust reporters—not until you know who puts the credits in their pockets."

Hatha watched Reyne for a brief moment before turning back to Sammy. "Let him land." She then turned to her guard. "Tully, have him brought to the control room. Have extra security on hand in case he tries something."

Sometime later, Willas James arrived with a cadre of camera handlers and Darion security forces.

Hatha moved to greet him first. "Willas James, it's a pleasure to meet you in person. I'm Hatha Satine, serving as interim stationmaster of Sol Base." She motioned to Reyne. "And, this is Marshal Aramis Reyne of the Fringe Liberation Campaign."

Willas shook both their hands. "I'm familiar with both of you. Thank you for allowing me to land."

"Why did you land?" Reyne asked bluntly. "Sol Base is about to become the most dangerous place to be in the Collective."

Willas grinned. "Which means it's the best place for a reporter to win a Halston Prize."

"True, though the CUF might not look too friendly on a reporter on the ground with torrents rather than up in the air on the *Unity*," Reyne said.

Willas looked offended. "I travel under the Fair News and Reporting Act. I report the news, and I go where the news is." He paused. "And I'm down here because Corps General Laciam wouldn't return my comm request."

Reyne smiled when the reporter said something that made the most sense about why he was in Sol Base.

Willas motioned to his camera handlers. "We're here to check things out firsthand. Is it true you have control of Sol Base?"

"It's true," Reyne said.

"The Darion people have reclaimed their colony," Hatha said.

"And what did you do with the CUF dromadiers who were here, as well as the crews of the ships above us?" Willas continued.

"They are being held as prisoners of war," Reyne said.

"I will give you a tour, so you can see all prisoners are being treated with respect."

"I would like that," Willas said. "Does that mean you took control of Sol Base without the loss of any lives?"

"Unfortunately, lives were lost on both sides," Hatha said.

"Four dromadiers and fifty-eight colonists were killed on the ground, and we estimate three hundred and twenty-six dromadiers and thirteen colonists were killed in the air when Commandant Corll refused to stand down and negotiate. But those numbers will pale compared to the number of deaths if the *Unity* fires upon Sol Base, where there are over fifteen thousand innocents working at rebuilding the colony and shipping food to the Collective."

"Speaking of food," Willas continued, "will you cut off food to Alluvia and Myr, now that you're in control of Sol Base?"

"Absolutely not," Hatha said. "However, that's not up to me. I have transports sitting in Sol Base's docks right now, loaded with food, and they can't launch without risk of being shot down. I'm not going to risk the lives of colonists to have them try to sneak around a CUF blockade. Perhaps citizens will risk their lives to attempt circumventing the blockade."

"Stationmaster," Sammy announced. "The *Unity* has reached our airspace and has sent a comm request."

"I want to report this live," Willas said. "Do you have a problem with that?"

"No. I want the Collective to see what we've been facing," Hatha said.

Reyne said nothing, though his jaw was clenched tight. He didn't like reporters. They played with words and used video snippets to tell the story they were getting paid to tell. Reporters had made the torrents out to be the aggressors in the Uprising, and they'd done the same in the Campaign. He believed Willas James would be no different.

Willas tapped his wrist comm. "Hey, Sydney, I'm going to be sending you a live feed. Have Hanna start with the live feed and be ready to cut to me... Where am I? I'm at Sol Base, which has been taken by colonists, and Corps General Laciam has just arrived on the *Unity*... Yes, I'm serious. Drop everything else and slate me in for at least the next hour... Trust me, this will be a big story." Willas lowered his wrist comm and looked back to Hatha and Reyne.

Sammy opened the comm request, and Corps General Laciam's face appeared on the comm screen. Reyne made certain to stand out of the camera's field, and Hatha stepped closer to the screen.

"I am Corps General Laciam with the CUF *Unity*. You have seized unauthorized control of Sol Base and are hereby ordered to surrender immediately."

"Hello, Corps General. I am Hatha Satine, and I have been serving as interim stationmaster since the station was opened following the blight. I did not *seize* Sol Base. The Darion people held peaceful protests across the colony, and they were fired upon. My security forces arrested those responsible for killing unarmed people. The incident would've been over except that your Commandant Corll attempted to bypass legal standards and attacked the colony. We defended ourselves and acquired control of the *Littorio* and the *Houston* as a result."

"Those ships are the property of the Collective Unified Forces and must be returned immediately."

"Corps General, it's my job to do what I have to do to ensure the space docks are operational. I did what I believed needed to be done to protect the docks and innocent lives."

Laciam guffawed. "No. You participated in a wartime event, leading an attack on my ships and people, which makes you a torrent. I know Aramis Reyne is there. Put him onscreen."

Hatha sighed and took a dramatic step back.

Reyne stepped forward. "Corps General."

Laciam scowled. "Aramis Reyne, you are a war criminal, and you have willfully attacked the lawful protectors of the Collective. Your actions have led to the deaths of citizens and colonists alike. You will be judged for your crimes."

Reyne cocked his head. "You said it yourself: we're at war. I know who I fight for. I fight for the colonies, trying to protect them from getting blown up or from getting hit by the blight again—both of which were delivered by the ship you're now commanding. I fight to keep colonists from being shot during peaceful protests. Tell me, who do you fight for?"

"I fight for the Collective, of course, while you fight for secession from the Collective. You are a criminal whose actions have cost the Collective trillions. And now, you attempt to close off Sol Base—which means all of Darios—from the Collective. Sol Base is a territory of the Collective, and I will do whatever is needed to protect all the parts from its enemies."

Reyne held up a hand. "We're currently managing Sol Base with nonviolent force. That will change if you start shooting at us. Every shot you fire, you also risk shooting citizens currently in custody. Your own dromadiers are stationed on the *Littorio* and they, too, are here to protect Sol Base."

Laciam squinted then he chortled. "Conscripts." He practically spat out the word. "You have ten minutes to surrender yourself and peacefully turn Sol Base over to the rightful authorities, or you will be fired upon."

"Sol Base is already with its rightful authorities. It's with the Darions, not torrents, not dromadiers, *Darions.*"

"You now have nine minutes."

The screen went blank.

Immediately, Reyne heard Willas speaking behind him. He turned to see the reporter with his back to Reyne and facing cameras. Reyne stepped out of the camera fields, but he suspected at least one camera had been on him the entire time and likely still was.

"Well, so much for negotiating," Reyne said as Hatha stepped closer to him.

"He didn't say if he'd fire on the ships or on us," Hatha said.

"I'd lay bets he's trying to zero in on where I'm located," Reyne said. He turned to Sammy. "Did you make sure the *Littorio* and the *Houston* got all that?"

"Every second you two were on with Laciam, they saw, too," Sammy replied.

"Marshal Reyne, a question," Willas called out.

Reyne waved him off, walked over to Sixx, and took a seat. "That could've gone better," Sixx said.

"Stationmaster Satine," Willas said. "How are you going to respond to the Corps General's ultimatum: surrender or be fired upon?"

"I certainly hope he doesn't fire upon Sol Base," Hatha said. "It's not only the bread and butter of the Collective, it's also my home. If he destroys the docks, everyone starves. There's no way around that."

As Willas and Hatha continued their discussion, Reyne spoke quietly to Sixx. "He's not bluffing. I hate to say this, but I'm thinking we raise the white flag."

"You do that, and the crews of *Crazy's Coral* and *Blue Jay* and all the other colonists who gave up their lives won't mean a thing." Sixx leaned forward. "Listen, we both knew it was a gamble going for Sol Base, but I think we've got to hold on to it. Let them bomb the docks. Then the citizens starve. We've still got New Sol."

"It's not big enough to feed half the colonies, let alone Myr and Alluvia," Reyne countered.

"Like I said, let the citizens starve. We'll figure out something for the colonies. We always do."

Reyne leaned back and rubbed his temples. He'd been counting on the fact that the CUF would negotiate, at least for the return of their crews and ships. Sol Base was crucial to the Collective. When it'd been hit by the blight and shipments were halted for nearly a month, the Collective had been thrown into a recession. Another month was all they needed before citizens would force Parliament to step in. Reyne hadn't been able to buy a full week.

He pushed back to his feet, feeling every day of his sixty-seven years.

"Three minutes," Sammy called out.

Reyne approached Hatha and Willas.

"Marshal Reyne," Willas began. "Stationmaster Satine says she won't surrender Darios to the Collective Unified Forces, or to what she's called 'bullies.' What do you say?"

Reyne looked at her, a bit surprised at her response. He turned to Willas. "She's right. The Collective has become a schoolyard, and colonists are tired of getting beat up and having all their stuff stolen. I'll defend Sol Base until my dying breath."

The comm screen chimed.

"Put him on," Reyne said, and he approached the screen. Meanwhile, he could hear Willas continuing his broadcast behind him.

"Your time is up. This is your last chance to surrender," Laciam said.

"Sol Base belongs to the Darions. I can't surrender their colony. There are lives at stake, both citizens and colonists. If you fire—"

The screen went blank.

Reyne spun around. "Where'd he go?"

"He disconnected," Sammy said.

"Tell the ships to put their shields up."

"The *Unity* has fired their phase cannons at Sol Base," Sammy announced.

Willas began speaking louder into the cameras, but Reyne ignored him.

"Where's it going to hit?" he asked.

Sammy started to answer, but he was cut off by a deafening sound. The ground quaked, and Reyne found himself knocked to the floor, covered by Sixx. When the vibrations stopped, Sixx helped Reyne to his feet. Dust flitted in the air, and two of the comm screens were cracked.

"That was close," Sixx muttered. "You okay, boss?"

"Yeah."

"I can't believe it. The *Unity* fired upon us! This is Willas James of DZ-Five News. I'm standing here with my crew in the Sol Base station. As you can see, the blast just missed us. There are broken screens around me and chairs knocked to the floor..."

Reyne was impressed to see the reporter and his camera handlers on their feet and reporting so quickly after an attack. "Sammy, where'd they hit?"

"One hit the station, obviously. At least two hit Main Street, and, oh crap, one hit the docks. It looks like an entire concourse has been taken out."

"No," Hatha said, as Tully held her in place. "He can't bomb the docks."

"He can and he did," Reyne said.

The cracked comm screen chimed.

Reyne's lips thinned. "Put him on screen."

The crack down the middle of the screen set apart the two halves of Laciam's face, making him resemble Frankenstein's monster. The Myrad seemed pleased with himself. "As an act of mercy, I give you one more chance. Surrender, or you will be killed."

Reyne glanced at Hatha, who gave him a hard look. He turned to Laciam. "Never. Sol Base belongs to the Darions."

"So be it," Laciam said, and the screen went blank once again.

Reyne turned to face the others in the room. Willas, who was still speaking rapidly into the camera, was the only one who didn't look at him with dread.

"I wish we were at New Sol right about now," Sixx said drily.

Wrist comms chimed, and Reyne noticed Willas and his entire cadre all glancing down at theirs at the same time.

After a quick pause, Willas continued speaking, evidently still on live feed. "I've just been informed that we're now cutting over to Senator Etzel at an emergency Parliament session. He will be broadcasting live, across all channels. If you don't hear from me again, that means Sol Base has been destroyed. Take care, and stay safe, everyone."

As soon as the camera cut, Willas waved his hand in a circle. "Hurry and pull up the feed."

"I have it up," a handler said. She turned around her camera and tapped a couple buttons, and then the feed displayed on the comm screen. Senator Etzel, perhaps the oldest of all the senators, stood at a podium in a building Reyne did not recognize. His speech was already underway.

"... the Collective is greater than the sum of its parts. The loss of any single territory can cause irreparable damage to our way of life. If the war continues, we will lose Sol Base, if we haven't already, and the remaining fringe stations will soon follow the same tragic path. Therefore, Parliament has called for an immediate armistice so that we may discuss options with Seda Faulk and representatives of the colonies. We have informed Corps General Laciam of our intentions, and I, along with several representatives of Parliament, will be leaving immediately to travel to Darios. It is our hope that we can end this war and bring peace to the Collective."

Etzel stepped down from the podium, and a press secretary

stepped up to take questions. Reyne looked around him, taking in the silence. "You hear that?"

"You mean the sound of us not getting blown up?" Sixx said.

After a moment, Hatha giggled and cupped her hands to her lips. She then turned to the reporter. "Willas James, I think you just saved all our lives."

Willas smiled proudly. "I just report the news."

"You'll also likely get a Halston," one of his handlers joked.

"Still dislike reporters?" Sixx asked Reyne quietly.

"They're growing on me."

CHAPTER 19

THE CONCEPT OF PEACE

Sol Base, Darios

SEDA LANDED at the Sol Base docks the morning of the meeting. Tax and Corbin stepped out of the ship first. Seda disliked all the safety precautions he'd been forced to take, but he had no other choice when the CUF wanted him dead. When Tax signaled that the area looked safe, he emerged to find Hari and Reyne waiting for him.

He smiled, embracing each. "It's good to see you both unharmed."

"We're luckier than others were," Reyne said.

Seda sobered. "I saw the damage from above. How many lives were lost in the bombing?"

"Not as many as there could've been. We're still cleaning up debris, so we don't have a hard number, but it's looking like around eighty killed in the phase cannon blasts."

"Their deaths shouldn't have happened, but if that's what it took to get Parliament's attention, then their sacrifice may save thousands of lives."

Hari motioned to the waiting vehicle. "Come. We're meeting at the fringe station. Hatha's hosting."

The group climbed into the luxury Rosten. As they rode from the space docks to the fringe station, Reyne updated Seda on details not yet covered on their daily check-ins.

"So, the *Littorio* and the *Houston* are ready to defend Sol Base should this meeting turn to shit?

Reyne nodded. "Both are fully crewed with conscripts who had been serving on board and backfilled with torrents who've served on those ships before. We have good crews. The problem is, they have to keep several major systems offline so the CUF can't take remote control of the ships. That means communications can only be handled via wrist comms."

"It's better than not having the ships at all," Seda said. "Without them, Laciam could've swooped in and taken Sol Base back without bombing."

"I'm not so sure they made any difference," Hari chimed in. "I think Laciam is hotheaded enough that he wanted to show off his power."

Seda chuckled drily. "He sounds like a younger version of Ausyar."

Hari nodded. "I think that's exactly what he is, which means we will always have a delicate dance with the CUF, regardless of how today goes."

"We're here," Tax said. "That's a lot more droms than I was expecting."

Seda looked out the window to see at least ten squads of dromadiers moving about the outside of the station. Darion security forces moved toward the vehicle and formed a wall between the Rosten's occupants and the droms. Tax and Corbin stepped out to converse with the soldiers.

"Laciam notified us he was sending them down to ensure security was in place for Etzel's arrival," Reyne said. "I told him one transport would be allowed to land, and he must've packed them in there like bunks on a frigate. Good thing we're still in control of the docks. Otherwise, Laciam would have droms crawling all over Sol Base by now."

"It's a thin line we're walking, and anyone can see that. Laciam knows he can take Sol Base any time he wants it, but he'll lose the docks—either by blowing them himself or by us blowing them."

Reyne chuckled. "Don't tell Hatha that. If she thought we'd blow the docks, we'd be fighting her security forces as well."

"Oh, I'm sure Hatha sees our predicament," Seda mused. "I've known her long enough to know she doesn't miss much."

He stepped out of the vehicle and strode toward the station. Reyne walked alongside, and Tax, Corbin, and Hari formed a perimeter of sorts around them, encircled by the Darions. Seda had been to the fringe station dozens of times in his career, but this was the first time he'd been there since the blight was dropped on the colony. Except for a blackened, bombed section off to his left that was marked off, the station looked unchanged but felt entirely different. While there were people moving about, there were nowhere near the numbers that had been there a year before. The station lacked vibrancy. He hoped, over time, the colony would fully repopulate.

Darions led them down the hallway to the right, and they reached a conference room Seda had often sat in for meetings with other Collective business leaders. Several people were already inside. Reyne broke off to talk with Sixx.

Hatha looked up as the group entered. "Ah, Seda!" She walked over to greet him.

Seda smiled and embraced her. "Hatha, it's been far too long."

"It has. It shouldn't take a war to bring you to Darios," she said.

He gave a slight bow. "My apologies. I've been a bit busy lately."

A clean-cut man approached, and Seda shook his hand. "Willas, I see you've been quite busy yourself."

Willas James smiled. "Just doing my job."

"And he's understating, terribly so," Hatha said. "This man and his camera crew prevented Sol Base from being utterly destroyed. I think he deserves to wear one of those torrent teardrops you each wear around your necks."

Willas held up his hands. "Oh, no. I'm no torrent. I report the news, and I leave it to my audience to decide what to do with the information. The number one rule in the news is that reporters don't pick sides."

"Your predecessor picked a side," Seda countered.

"True, Lina Tao picked a side," Willas said. "And she ended up dead because of it. As for me, I prefer to keep both my job and my life as long as possible."

One of Hatha's assistants approached. "Excuse me, Stationmaster, gentlemen. Senator Etzel's ship has landed."

Seda rubbed his hands together. "Then we'd better get our ducks in a row."

Thirty minutes later, Senator Etzel arrived with a sizable entourage. Seda recognized several senators and was glad to see Parliament at least pretending to play along. Whether they were serious about ending the war or simply biding time for a full-blown CUF invasion remained to be seen.

"Senators," Seda said, and he went through the formalities of greeting each one. Barrett Anders entered behind them, and Seda smiled, holding out a hand. "It's good to see you again, Commandant."

Anders smirked. "It's Corps General once again, Mr. Faulk. Commandant Laciam is taking leave, and I'm serving in his stead."

Senator Etzel stepped in. "Corps General Anders's role will be made official and permanent at the next Parliamentary session. My associates and I believe Barrett Anders better encompasses our vision. While Maximus Laciam is an excellent officer, he represented the viewpoint of Senator Heid, who may not necessarily be aligned with the vision of Parliament."

"Excellent decision, Senator." Ah, so the senators had already begun to roll back Heid's decisions. His control over Parliament seemed to be coming to an end, now that the puppet master had been removed from his puppets.

Seda motioned to Hatha. "Stationmaster Hatha Satine has graciously hosted us today, so shall we take advantage of the time and facilities she's given us and begin?"

The leaders sat around the large conference table, filling every seat. Hatha sat next to Seda, and he shot Reyne a glance to make sure he sat on Seda's other side and across from Anders. Willas James stood in the corner, his camera handlers stationed at different places across the room.

Upon seeing Willas, Etzel frowned. "I'm not comfortable with a reporter recording sensitive negotiations. The things we discuss may be confidential or inflammatory if portrayed in the wrong light."

"Understood," Seda said. "Willas James is a Collective news reporter, so I should be the one bothered." Etzel opened his mouth to object, but Seda continued. "Citizen James has assured me that he will not be sending a live feed to his station. He will not broadcast the story until our meeting is done today. This could be a monumental moment in Collective history. Don't you agree that having the media record it for posterity is a good thing?"

Etzel pointed at James. "I need to see your story before you run it."

James nodded. "Everyone can see my story before I send it, but I won't change it."

"I wouldn't ask you to," Etzel said, though it sounded like Etzel would do exactly that.

"Shall we get down to business?" Seda asked.

"Yes. Certainly." Etzel clasped his hands together on the table. "I'd like to begin by stating how important each colony is to the Collective, and I will do everything in my power to deliver a positive outcome to all members, regardless of their legal status. The loss of Sol Base's space docks would cut off food supplies for over a year while new docks are built. Hundreds of thousands of people would starve if that happened. I think we both agree that no one can afford to have Sol Base's docks destroyed during this war. Therefore, I'm here to offer terms of peace for Darios."

Seda leaned forward with a slanted smile. "Senator, we're not here to talk about Darios. We're here to talk about the independence of all four colony planets."

"Perhaps it's best we discuss Darios first. Then we can discuss each planet in turn."

"Or, we could begin with the cease-fire signed by Corps General Anders and myself."

"That agreement was developed with neither Parliament's input nor approval," Etzel said. "The treaty was skewed too heavily in favor of the colonies and would wreak havoc on Alluvia and Myr's economic systems."

Seda cocked his head. "What were the sticking points, then? Let's discuss those."

Etzel sighed. "The very basis of the document. It states that each colony planet would no longer be a part of the Collective."

"Yes, however, we'd ensure fair trade agreements are developed," Seda said.

"Trade agreements mean little if you control the space docks," Etzel countered.

"If I may," Anders interjected. "In the cease-fire, we established that the fringe stations would be required to maintain open trade with Myrad and Alluvian traders alike, with guaranteed annual minimum quantities and negotiated fair rates for each planet, along with an option to reevaluate trade agreements after an established duration."

"That, however, still keeps the fringe stations under the control of the colony," Etzel said.

"Not if we split ownership," Hatha said.

Seda jerked to face her.

She continued. "What if a wing of the Sol Base station and a concourse of the docks remains under Collective ownership? And the colony owns the remaining portions."

"The Collective owns half of the station and docks, along with access—with immunity—on all major roads and airspaces. After all, owning a dock does us little good if our ships or goods are seized as soon as we leave."

"Half is impractical and just plain greedy," Hatha said. "The Collective is essentially Alluvia and Myr. That's two worlds compared with the four worlds and asteroid belt I need to continue to serve. One concourse to the Collective, and that leaves two concourses for me to manage."

"You're assuming every colony planet will leave the Collective," Etzel said. "We haven't discussed them yet."

"Then we'll readjust the ownership based on who remains in the Collective," she said.

"No," Seda said slowly and firmly.

Everyone turned to him.

"One concourse and one wing at Sol Base. The other colony worlds will not be bartering pieces today."

Hatha gave him a nod in agreement before she turned back to Etzel. "No adjustments. And I support the access you request on the ground and in the air as long as all travelers—

regardless of which banner they fly—obey interplanetary laws."

Seda set his hands on the table. "Senator Etzel, what do you have to say to what Hatha's offering?"

"We'll need to work out the details this week, but it sounds possible," Etzel said. "However, we need the ability to build future space docks in new locations on the colony worlds."

Seda spoke. "That's for you and the colony's leaders to work out when the time comes. That's not on the table today."

Etzel frowned but accepted the statement with a nod.

"I have a proposal." Seda motioned to Hatha's assistant, who'd been jotting notes on the original cease-fire as they spoke. Small screens extended upward from the table. "Here's the revised treaty. It states all the colony worlds are independent of the Collective, with new wording to cover shared ownership of space docks associated with each fringe station. Everything else is left as previously written, including the bit on guaranteed trade quantities and rates."

"I haven't even had a chance to read this yet," Etzel said.

Seda tried not to let his impatience show. "You probably have the cease-fire agreement memorized, and the revisions are clearly marked. What's left on the table that you think is missing?"

"For one, there's nothing in here regarding taxes paid to the Collective. We depend on that money."

Seda chuckled. "There will be no taxes paid to the Collective by worlds no longer a part of the Collective. That's the whole concept of independence. Now, you can make up some of that money through tariffs and sales taxes and other ways, which I'm sure you'll have no problem inventing."

Etzel scowled. "Alluvia and Myr depend on those taxes. What you're proposing will eliminate citizens' guaranteed income."

"Yes, they'll have to work for a living, just like colonists have always done." Seda then gave him a hard look. "We can discuss minor details, but I want to make sure you understand, Senator. *All* colonies must be independent. That is non-negotiable. We can talk about each one separately if you want, but the outcome will be the same: they will all be free. If, at some point, they decide to rejoin the Collective, that's between them and you. If you can't accept that, then we do not need to spend further time negotiating. That means the war goes on, and we'll both lose the Sol Base docks."

Etzel's lips thinned. The pair faced off for several minutes without speaking.

Finally, Etzel broke. "We will accept the peace treaty. However, we want everything laid out specifically: which concourses, which parts of the stations, parcels of land that those items sit upon, and so on."

"We can work out those details this week, as I also have a few things to add, such as ensuring space sectors remain neutral," Seda said.

Etzel nodded. "I also have a few terms of peace you must address."

"I expected as much," Seda said. "What are these terms you speak of?"

"Senator Heid must be returned, unharmed."

"He will be, *after* his trial," Seda said.

Etzel's gaze narrowed. "I need your assurance that you will not carry out his punishment, whatever your judge or jury deem for him. If he is found guilty of war crimes by an Alluvian court, you must trust that Parliament will see he faces a punishment fitting the standards of his home world.

Which meant Heid would never see the inside of a prison cell, let alone a firing squad, once he returned home. However, Seda still had a few strings on Alluvia left that he could pull. He'd ensure Heid would not get away with his crimes for long.

"As soon as Gabriel Heid's trial is held and broadcast, I will see that he is safely returned to Alluvia."

Etzel motioned to Anders, who then spoke. "Now, we must speak of any CUF property you have in your possession, as well as all prisoners of war you're holding."

"The *Littorio* and the *Houston* will be returned to you after you sign the treaty and today's outcomes are shared across the Collective by Citizen James."

Anders smiled. "I'm looking forward to getting my ship back. And the prisoners?"

"As for prisoners of war, all, including Commandant Corll and Captain Singh, will be returned, unharmed, at a time and location when and where you return all colonists you've been holding as prisoners and all conscripts, who are to be immediately freed from service."

Etzel gave a small jolt when Seda mentioned the conscripts, clearly a factor Etzel had not yet taken into consideration.

Anders nodded. "We can work out a neutral location in which to make the exchange."

After another hour of making compromises, the attendees took a break. Etzel and his entourage left the meeting room. Willas went to work recording his broadcast.

Hatha stood. "I need a drink."

Seda leaned back in his chair and glanced at Reyne. "You stayed awfully quiet."

Reyne shrugged. "I would've spoken up if I thought we were getting screwed, but honestly, they capitulated on your demands a lot more than I ever expected them to."

Seda gave a dark smile. "That's because they came here to surrender, and we let them do it gracefully."

CHAPTER 20

GHOST TOWN CELEBRATIONS

Rebus Station, Terra

CRITCH HAD JUST LINED up the shot when someone tapped his shoulder, throwing off his aim. He snarled. "Do that again, and you lose a kneecap."

"The war's over!" Mick said. "It's on all the channels. Parliament signed a treaty. The colonies are free!"

Critch frowned. "No shit?"

Mick held out his wrist comm. "See for yourself."

He watched the video play and read the closed captioning on the small screen. It was that DZ-Five News reporter, and he was standing next to some senators, and sure as shit, both Seda and Reyne were there. It looked like a political circus, but it also looked like the real thing.

"We're free! The droms are supposed to clear out of every colony immediately."

He turned back to the droms on the street below. The squad was moving toward their vehicle, firing haphazardly. A colonist was caught by a shot and fell. Critch lined up his shot once more and fired. The drom went down.

"Why'd you do that? The war's over," Mick said.

"He didn't get the message," Critch replied. He aimed at the squad again, but they were now safe in their vehicle.

He pushed himself into a seated position, set down his rifle, and looked at his wrist comm. He tapped out a note and broadcast it to everyone on his contact list who was currently on Terra. He wrote:

War is over. We won. Watch your backs until CUF leaves.

There. He didn't want to lose any torrents to thinking that just because a war was officially over, the bloodshed was over. The two rarely went hand in hand.

He pushed to his feet and turned to the torrent with him. "Let's head to the docks and make sure they leave with their tails between their legs."

Mick grinned. "You got it."

The pair made their way to the space docks, careful to avoid CUF vehicles and squads even though the gunfire had stopped. Colonists stood on the streets, cheering their newfound independence. Critch thought they were foolish to be outside so soon when blasters were still warm from firing. But he understood why they were there. This was a day they'd only dreamed of living to see. Hell, Critch even felt a bit choked up.

By the time they reached the docks, half of the CUF transports were already gone and the rest were being loaded. Terran conscripts were being left on the ramps with nothing but the clothes on their backs. But they didn't seem to mind. They ran onto the crowded walkways and cheered, along with thousands of intrepid colonists there to see the dromadiers leave their colony.

As soon as the transports were gone and the warship left Terra's airspace, Critch sent out teams to check tunnels and buildings for any droms who may have been left behind. Fortunately, the CUF had done a good job of taking their citizens home.

When daytime cheers morphed into nighttime celebrations, Critch grabbed a truck and made his way to the apartment building on the other side of town. He parked across the street and climbed the stairs. Doors were open, and people were smiling as they toasted one another with shots of Terran whiskey—likely home brewed. He stopped at a door and pulled out a new wrist comm. He knocked. When there was no answer, he stepped inside to find it empty. Not that he was surprised. The kid would be out celebrating independence day with his friends. He set the wrist comm on the counter. He left no note—Kassel would know whom it was from.

Critch returned to his truck and decided to make one final stop at the checkpoint he'd passed through earlier with Kassel to confirm the two conscripts had made it out okay. He slowed as he approached. A bombed-out CUF vehicle still smoked at the checkpoint, and he saw two slumped shapes on the ground.

He swallowed, stopped the truck, and climbed out with heavy steps. He recognized the conscripts through their burned hair and blackened faces. Their boots and gear were missing, likely scavenged within minutes of their deaths. The smoke meant they couldn't have been dead for more than several hours. They'd likely been killed after the war ended. *What a waste.*

He came down on a knee and placed a hand on each shoulder. "May you find peace in the Eversea."

He pushed to his feet with a sigh. He'd about turned to go when he saw another shape mostly hidden by the vehicle. He approached. Dread clenched his jaw shut. Like the women, Kassel had been killed by the explosion. His chest and face were bloody from shrapnel. And, like the women, Kassel's shoes were missing and the contents of his backpack were strewn on the stone road. It looked like anything valuable was gone, with only wrappers and trinkets left behind.

Critch grimaced as he picked up the small toy spaceship from the ground. Of course Kassel had kept the ship. He reminded Critch of himself at that age. Overconfident and determined to be the best pilot in the system. For the first time in years, he felt a tear on his cheek. He gently placed the ship in a pocket on his bag. He slung the bag over his shoulder and then bent down and scooped up the teenager's body in his arms.

He carried Kassel to the truck and drove out of the colony, where he gave the kid a proper Terran cremation.

Several hours later, fatigued and dirty, Critch returned to Rebus Station and tracked down Miko at the Last Drop Café. Someone held out a drink, and Critch ignored it.

He walked straight toward Miko's table, where the captain sat with his crew, enjoying a much-needed break.

Miko's grin fell as soon as he saw Critch's expression.

"We need to head out," Critch said.

Miko downed the rest of his drink in a single gulp. "Where to?"

"Nova Colony. I have some unfinished business."

Devil Town, Spate

"We're all set," Birk said. "Operation Devil's Playground launches in an hour."

Throttle grinned. "It's about time. I can't wait to see the look on their faces when we—"

"Throttle! Birk!" Garrett came running into the brothel room where they'd been holed up for nearly a week.

Throttle frowned. She'd never seen Garrett run before, at

least not without being shot at. She reached for her blaster. "What's wrong?"

"Nothing! It's over! The war is over! The droms are pulling out as we speak."

She stiffened. "What do you mean it's over?"

Garrett rushed over to the wall screen and turned on the news channel. A news reporter was talking about the colonies being independent. In the background, she saw Reyne standing with Seda and a bunch of uppity-looking folks.

"He pulled it off," she said on an exhalation. Her smile morphed into a frown. "Aw, hell."

"What's wrong?" Birk asked.

She turned to him. "That means we can't carry out Operation Devil's Playground."

He laughed.

"It was going to be legendary," she said.

He kissed her. "Don't worry. I'm sure we'll get to fight droms again."

She scowled. "I kind of hope so."

CHAPTER 21

RETRIBUTION

Nova Colony within the Space Coast asteroid belt

CRITCH ENTERED Nova Colony's tunnels. He'd grown up in the colony with his sister and best friend, led it as a pirate for nearly two decades, and could find his way through the maze-like tunnel system blindfolded. Kora had been killed when the CUF invaded Nova Colony nearly twenty-five years ago. Chutt had at least managed to get off that rock with Critch, only to be killed on Terra. As he walked, faces of those who'd died went through his mind. There'd been so many. Yet he still lived, a soldier of retribution.

He wanted to quit... quit the fighting, quit the killing. But he couldn't; not as long as those lived who sought to suffocate others beneath shrouds of righteousness. He trudged on.

When he arrived at the prison cells, he continued until he reached the maximum security cell at the end of the line.

The guard sitting near the door rushed to his feet as soon as he saw who approached. "Are you here to see the prisoner?"

Critch nodded. "Give me ten minutes alone with him."

"I'm not supposed to—" Critch's hard look cut him off. "Sure, no problem."

"Why don't you take a break?" Critch offered. "Ten minutes."

The guard nodded and then strode away.

Critch looked through the tiny window in the door to see Heid sitting on the bed, his legs crossed in a meditative pose. The older man looked at peace.

Critch made no attempts to be quiet as he opened the door and stepped inside. He set down the small box he'd been carrying and faced the prisoner.

Heid opened his eyes. "You have questions you wish to ask me before my trial tomorrow?"

"Hm."

Heid watched him for a lengthy moment. "Ah, you're not here to ask questions then."

"Remember what I told you the day you killed Demes?"

Heid eyed the scabbard at Critch's hip before returning his direct gaze. "I believe you warned me that you would take my head."

Critch pulled out the sword.

Heid, slowly and methodically, pushed to his feet. He opened his mouth to speak—

Critch swung the sword and took Heid's head off with a single, smooth strike. The head bounced on the mattress as the rest of the body toppled to the floor. Critch set the head upright on the center of the bed before turning back to the body. With another swing, he cut off Heid's right hand. He placed the hand in the box and wiped his sword on the blanket before sheathing it. Then he strode from the cell, leaving the door wide open.

The guard was returning as Critch left, and Critch tilted his head toward him when they met in the hallway. Each continued on their way. Critch wasn't worried about getting arrested.

Nearly everyone who worked at Nova Colony was still on his payroll.

He headed back up to the main hallway. There, he stopped by the post office. He set down the box on the counter and wrote a name, *Senator Liu*, on a slip of paper. He pushed it across the table, leaving a smeared trail of blood. The agent looked at it and then at him with fear.

"Package and ship that out with the next runner," he said.

She nodded and lifted the box as though she was afraid a monster would jump out of it and eat her.

He left and walked to the dock, for the first time bypassing the Uneven Bar. He donned a flight suit and crossed through the airlocks to enter the depressurized space docks. There, in zero-g, he pulled himself easily toward where the *Lady Lilith* waited, ready for takeoff. By the time he climbed on board and reached the bridge, the engines were powered up.

Domino gave him a nod as he entered. "We have a possible hit. Someone said they saw the *Honorless* docked at Devil Town, getting restocked."

Critch buckled in. "Let's go get my ship."

CHAPTER 22

NEW BEGINNINGS

Nova Colony, Space Coast

"CONGRATULATIONS, Seda, or should I call you, President Seda?" Reyne said, and then broke into a grin.

Seda shook his head. "Never call me that. I've always hated pomp and protocol."

"Oh, I think you like it better than you let on."

Seda pinched his fingers. "Maybe just a little, but don't tell anyone."

Reyne looked around the living room as he took a drink. There wasn't much décor and furniture, but what there was looked to be of the best quality—and definitely not cheap. "You know, this is my first time in Critch's residence. It's exactly what I expected."

A woman emerged from what Reyne believed to be Critch's bedroom. She strolled in, wearing only a robe, and grabbed a glass of water. She smiled warmly at the two men as she strolled seductively through the room. She ran a hand along Seda's shoulder as she walked by. "Coming back to bed?"

He reached out and kissed the back of her hand. "Soon, Layla. Soon."

Reyne smirked. "And that's not something I expected at all."

Seda smiled but said nothing.

"So, what will you do, now that you're the first president of the Alliance of Free Colonies?"

Seda's humor drained from his face. "Good question. There's so much work to do, I don't even know where to start. This isn't like starting a new company. We're talking about establishing governments for four independent worlds, *at the same time.* And, the Collective is not going to make any of it easy. Any delays in shipments or cost overages, and we'll be facing trouble with the CUF. Winning the war didn't end our troubles, not by a long shot; it just opened up an entirely new set of problems. We've still got to get colonists back to their homes, a memorial built on every world"—Seda took a long drink—"and then there's Critch..."

Reyne winced. "Yeah, how'd that conversation go with Etzel when you fed him the story about Heid hanging himself rather than facing shame back home?"

Seda chuckled. "He didn't buy the story for a second. He surprised me, though, when he didn't push it. I think he was glad he didn't have to deal with Heid again." Seda blew out a breath. "Critch is going to find himself back on top of the CUF's Most Wanted listed at the rate he's going."

Reyne grunted. "I think Critch has had that spot nailed for twenty years and counting."

"Cheers to that." Seda held up his glass, and they toasted.

After they drank, Seda spoke. "So, what's your plan after all this is done?"

"You mean, after the *Matador* ships?" Reyne shrugged. "I'm old. My bones ache. Maybe I'll retire."

Seda shot him a dubious look. "I don't see you retiring. It's just not in you."

"Well, I've considered going back to running mail."

Seda watched him for a moment. "Or, you could help me build the Alliance of Free Colonies. There's plenty of work, and I need leaders I can trust."

Reyne shook his head. "I'm not sure I'd be much good at politics."

"We need Playa's rilon production. We're rebuilding Ice Port, space docks and all. You grew up at the fringe station. Here's your chance to be a stationmaster at the new one."

Reyne watched him for a long while as he considered Seda's words. After a length, he spoke. "I'd consider it."

Sixx left Reyne with Seda. They'd be safe in Critch's residence and would be talking for hours. That gave Sixx time to take care of something he'd been putting off for far too long. He headed down Nova Colony's tunnels, all the way down to the prison. No guards were around—he'd checked to make sure they'd be on break. Many of the cells were empty; the ones with occupants were filled with drunks sleeping it off. He stopped at the only cell that didn't have a drunk in it.

Inside, Axos Wintsel lay on the bed, picking at his nails. Sixx pulled out a dagger. Axos had taken everything from Sixx, and the man hadn't even known or cared. Sixx and Qelle had been married only two years when the transport she was on disappeared. The authorities had told Sixx she was dead. He had never believed them. So he'd searched for years, meeting Reyne early on when he was at a low point. He'd never given up, but life had forced him to put his search on hold. While he lived free, Qelle had suffered in that man's house and died under his torture. She'd produced a daughter, and Sixx was thankful that at least a part of Qelle lived on in Lily.

He gripped the knife, took a deep breath, and then went to open the door.

"Sixx, don't."

He turned to see Bree walk toward him. "Stay out of this, Bree."

"I can't let you do this." Her face was stern, and he knew Bree could be as hardheaded as they came.

"You, of all people, know he's got to die. After what he did to you—to Qelle—to the others..."

"He can't hurt anyone anymore," she said quietly.

Sixx shook his head. "But what if he gets out?"

"He won't. No one knows he's here."

"We can't risk it," Sixx said.

She stepped closer and placed a hand on his cheek. "I can't risk what killing him will do to *you*."

He grunted. "You don't have to worry about me."

"I do, and I worry about the future you have with Lily."

He stiffened when Bree brought up the girl's name.

Bree continued. "She needs a father, and you would make a great father to her. But, what will you say when she asks what happened to her old father? What if she learns that you killed him?"

Sixx's jaw tightened. "But I made a promise to avenge Qelle."

Her chin lifted. "Then you'll have to decide what's more important: vengeance or Lily."

Sixx scowled.

Bree wrapped her hand over the one that held the blade. She gently pried it from his hand. With her other hand, she cupped his cheek, stepped on tiptoes, and kissed him. "Please," she said. "Sleep on it tonight; that's all I ask."

"It's that important to you?" he asked quietly.

She gave a small nod. "Lily needs a father; a *good* father."

He leaned his forehead against hers for a moment. He pulled back. "Tomorrow, then."

"Tomorrow," she echoed.

She stood there as he walked away.

She didn't follow, and he didn't stop, even though he knew why. He didn't even stop when he heard a cell door open. As the distance grew between them, he took the tunnels back up to the main thoroughfare and ended up at the Uneven Bar.

Reyne found him nursing a drink at a corner table.

"Well, it turns out Seda thinks I'd make a halfway decent stationmaster," Reyne said.

Sixx lifted a brow. "Oh? And what'd you say?"

"That I'd think on it." Reyne watched him for a length. His brow furrowed before he scowled. "You killed Axos."

Sixx shook his head and answered before taking a drink. "No."

Reyne looked confused. "So he's still alive?"

Sixx stared at his drink while he thought of Bree and of the knife she'd taken from him. A slow, sad smile emerged. "No."

Since the *Matador* had been reported to the CUF as being 'in pieces,' Reyne couldn't have it dock at any of the fringe stations, and it couldn't travel through the asteroid belt to dock at Nova Colony. That left it to sit in a sector the CUF rarely ventured out to, hidden and waiting for its new mission.

Transport ships were docked at nearly every one of its landing bays, each unloading dozens of colonists and all the possessions they were taking for the new journey.

Reyne stood on the bridge. Boden and Sixx had joined him as they waited for the ship's new captain and crew to arrive. A familiar sense of loss began building in Reyne's heart, the same he'd felt when Throttle took on her own ship. It was the worst feeling he'd ever experienced, and he never thought he'd have to endure it twice.

Throttle and Birk entered the bridge. Throttle's smile brightened Reyne's spirits, and he crossed the floor to embrace his daughter. "It's good to see you." He held her against him.

"You too, Dad."

He hated letting her go, but he did. He took a step back to give Sixx and Boden access to their former crew mate and family in all ways that mattered.

"Hey Kiddo," Sixx said before hugging her.

Boden was a bit awkward, but he then embraced her long and hard. And Reyne realized then that Boden knew he'd let the best thing that had ever happened to him get away.

"Hey, that's enough, big guy," Birk said, pulling the pair apart.

Throttle looked at the three men, focusing mostly on Reyne. "You know, it's still not too late for you to join us. And we've got room for the *Gryphon* in one of the landing bays."

Reyne forced a smile. "I'm too old to make the trip. No one needs to deal with my funeral out there."

Throttle's expression grew sad, and he could see she was fighting back tears.

"I'd go, but someone's got to keep your old man out of trouble," Sixx said. "Did you hear, he's going to take on the stationmaster job at Ice Port?"

Birk looked confused. "But there's no Ice Port."

"That makes it the easiest stationmaster job around then," Reyne said with a smile.

Boden opened his mouth, but Throttle shot up her hand. "Sorry, Boden. I love you to pieces, but we both know there's no good to come of you joining this crew."

Boden lowered his head in what may have been a nod.

"So, are you all ready for the trip?" Reyne asked quickly.

"Yeah," Throttle said, relieved for the change in topic. "We have our first twelve jumps programmed in. After that, it's all uncharted territory. Our juice will run out about two-thirds of the way into the trip, and then we'll coast on solar sails from there."

Sixx blew out a breath. "You've got guts, I'll give you that."

"It's really not so scary. I mean, think of all the satellites the Collective's been sending out for the past seven hundred or so years. We have a ton of data to work from. We have over two hundred habitable worlds mapped, and we're heading for the closest planet that's guaranteed to support life—that's *forty* light years out. Since we don't have the fuel for a return trip, we have to make the first one count."

"You have a name figured out for the new planet yet?"

"We have a few years to come up with that," Birk joked.

Reyne swallowed. "Send comm messages whenever you can. I know, without waypoints, there'll be lags, but still..."

"I'll send messages," she said quickly. "Just because I'm out of the system doesn't mean I'm gone forever."

It sure felt like she already was.

Reyne turned to Birk to change the subject. "You say goodbye to Critch yet?"

Birk nodded. "He wanted to see us off, but he couldn't make it. He was in the middle of a chase. He's hell-bent on getting the *Honorless* back. You know, *priorities*."

Reyne smirked. "It's his ship. I can understand." He paused to look around. "And, now this is *your* ship. What are you going to do with the *Scorpia*?"

Throttle and Birk looked at each other. Birk spoke first. "It was a gift from Critch, so we're keeping it. Taking it along." He motioned to the ship around them. "This one's such a beast, we figured the *Scorpia* might come in handy."

Throttle and Birk's wrist comms chimed at the same time. "Looks like the rest of the crew is on their way up. We'll have to go over some things with them before we make our spiel to the passengers."

"We'll leave you to it then," Reyne said, already feeling his feet become heavy.

"Wait, I got you a going away present," Sixx said. He turned around and grabbed a large box he had sitting on a chair. He brought it over and held it out. Birk took it with a frown. "What is it?"

Throttle's eyes grew wide. "Sixx, that's your biome kit."

Sixx shrugged. "I was saving it for my retirement on Spate or somewhere, but I figured you guys could probably find a use for it."

"I've never seen one of these before," Birk said in awe. "Does it seriously terraform an entire area?"

"It doesn't cover a planet, but it'd better get you a few good acres of edible food," Sixx said. "Otherwise, I went to a lot of trouble stealing that for nothing."

Throttle grinned. "Thanks, Sixx."

As people entered the bridge, Reyne knew the time had come. He grabbed Throttle once more and gave her a hug that he hoped conveyed all the love he felt for her. "Take care of yourself."

"I will. I love you, Dad," she said.

Reyne walked away and didn't care he was crying.

When Reyne, Sixx, and Boden reached the *Gryphon*, no one spoke. Reyne knew their hearts were breaking, too, and each took his own space.

Reyne backed the *Gryphon* out of the landing bay. Several of the transports had unloaded and had also detached from the colony ship. He reversed slowly to avoid a collision. As he passed the name, he paused.

"Well, would you look at that," Sixx said.

Reyne turned to see his friend join him on the bridge. He looked back at the name that had been painted over the old one: *GABRIELA*.

"You know, they named it because changing the *Matador* into a colony ship was her idea," Reyne said.

Sixx nodded. "It's a good name for a good ship and crew."

Reyne gave the colony ship one final look before he turned the *Gryphon* and prepped it for jump. He turned to Sixx. "Ready for our next adventure?"

Sixx grinned. "Hell, yes."

EPILOGUE

BARRETT ANDERS AWOKE with the feeling he was being watched. He reached to turn on the light, but a hand grabbed his wrist. He swung out with his other hand, only to be blocked.

"Don't fight," a male voice said.

The pressure released from his wrist, and Barrett pulled his hands back. The light came on, and he found a man covered in black from head to toe, save for his eyes. His irises were as dark as the assassin's garb he wore, and focused intently on Barrett.

Barrett sat up. "You're here to kill me," he said matter-of-factly.

The man watched him for a brief moment before saying, "No."

Barrett's gaze narrowed. "Why are you here, then?"

"I'm called Ranger." He pulled off his face mask. "I'm here to talk with you about the Founders..."

FRINGE LEGACY

Book 5 in the Fringe Series

After a bloody war, the colonies are free.

But they are not at peace.

The Alliance of Free Colonies is fragile and alluring to power-mongers. New enemies arise from around every corner, seeking to gain control of the now independent fringe stations. Assassinations, kidnappings, and murder become commonplace.

Aramis Reyne has dedicated himself to building a new station on the ice world of Playa. It's not easy, between battling the corporations for control and fending off attempts on his life. It gets worse when Critch goes missing, and Reyne learns of a new plot that could send the colonies spiraling back into war.

To save the Alliance, Reyne must infiltrate the Collective Unified Forces and make an impossible rescue.

The race is on and time is running out.

***

Read book 5, *Fringe Legacy*, today!

THE COLLECTIVE

The Collective is comprised of six terraformed planets in nearby solar systems within the Milky Way galaxy. The Collective is controlled by the dual leadership of Alluvia and Myr. Only those born on Alluvia and Myr are given legal status as citizens, while all others are considered colonists and receive fewer privileges. The Collective views colonists as means to achieve gain, and their pressure is driving the colonies—the fringe—to desperate actions.

MYR is a silver-rich, water-rich citizen world with idyllic islands. Myr was the first settled planet in the Collective. Myrads have argyria and take great pride in their blue-hued skin.

ALLUVIA is a water-covered citizen world and home to First City, the Collective's largest city. Alluvia was the second settled planet in the Collective, and has the highest gravity of all Collective worlds. Alluvia has thick cloud cover and frequent storms.

DARIOS is the most naturally habitable world and provides much of the Collective's food supply. As such, it's heavily regulated by the Collective. Its fringe station is Sol Base, which had been hit by the blight. Since then, the CUF has maintained a chokehold on Sol Base.

PLAYA is the furthest world from Alluvia and Myr. It has low gravity and freezing temperatures. Its fringe station is Ice Port, which was destroyed by the CUF. The Collective believes Playa to no longer be of value, now that its fringe station was destroyed. Unknown to the CUF, the torrent headquarters is here, located at Tulan Base, which has its own space dock.

SPATE is a desert-like world and has the largest fringe station, Devil Town, known for its massive indoor garden. Without a stationmaster, it is seen as neutral territory.

TERRA is a battle-scarred world, where much of the Fringe Liberation Campaign now takes place. Its fringe station is Rebus Station. Terra, the planet nearest to Alluvia and Myr, stands between the citizen worlds and Darios, making it a key planet in the Campaign. The torrent headquarters on Terra are located within Seda Faulk's secret retreat and space dock.

SPACE COAST is an asteroid belt outside Collective control and home to smugglers, pirates, and other outlaws. Its fringe station is Nova Colony. The CUF initiated a blockade when the Fringe Liberation Campaign began.

ABOUT THE AUTHOR

Rachel Aukes is the award-winning author of over thirty novels, including *100 Days in Deadland*, which made Suspense Magazine's Best of the Year list. She is also a Wattpad Star, her stories having over seven million reads. When not writing, she can be found flying old airplanes over the Midwest countryside and catering to an exceptionally spoiled fifty-pound lapdog.

Join Rachel's spam-free newsletter to be the first to hear about new releases: www.rachelaukes.com/join

ACKNOWLEDGEMENTS

With extreme thanks to my editors, Stephanie Riva and Laurel Kriegler, for helping make this story shiny; and to my jack-of-all-trades, Rob Shores, for catching the little things that could cause big problems. Thanks to Walter Scott for the feedback and ideas. Thank you to the Early Reader Brigade for giving an untested book a read. Most of all, thank you, my readers, for your messages, cheers, and enthusiasm.